THE MZUNGU BOY

MEJA MWANGI

THE MZUNGU BOY

A GROUNDWOOD BOOK
HOUSE OF ANANSI PRESS
TORONTO BERKELEY

Copyright © 1990, 2005 by Meja Mwangi
First North American edition 2005

No part of this publication may be reproduced, stored in a retrieval system or
transmitted, in any form or by any means, without the prior written consent of the
publisher or a licence from The Canadian Copyright Licensing Agency (Access
Copyright). For an Access Copyright licence, visit www.accesscopyright.ca or call
toll free to 1-800-893-5777.

Groundwood Books / House of Anansi Press
720 Bathurst Street, Suite 500, Toronto, Ontario M5S 2R4

Distributed in the USA by Publishers Group West
1700 Fourth Street, Berkeley, CA 94710

We acknowledge for their financial support of our publishing
program the Canada Council for the Arts, the Government of Canada through
the Book Publishing Industry Development Program (BPIDP) and the
Ontario Arts Council.

ONTARIO ARTS COUNCIL
CONSEIL DES ARTS DE L'ONTARIO

Library and Archives Canada Cataloging in Publication
Mwangi, Meja
The Mzungu Boy / Meja Mwangi.
Previously published under title: Little white man.
ISBN 0-88899-653-5 (bound).   ISBN 0-88899-664-0 (pbk.)
I. Mwangi, Meja. Little white man. II. Title.
PZ7.M974Mz 2005   j823'.914   C2004-906454-1

Printed and bound in Canada

One

I am not certain when I first heard the word mau-mau. It may have been during the first round-up, after Bwana Ruin's gun disappeared and was said to have been stolen by the mau-mau.

That fateful morning we had woken up to find our village surrounded by soldiers. Hundreds upon hundreds of heavily armed white soldiers. They rounded us all up — every man, woman and child — and herded us into the cattle auction pen outside the village. There they made us sit on fresh cow dung to wait for Bwana Ruin.

Meanwhile, they searched the village. They searched every single hut. They searched every nook and cranny. The villagers had received their monthly pay the night before. Many of them had hidden their money, but the soldiers unearthed it all. Later we learned that the soldiers had also stolen watches and jewelry.

They kept us in the cattle enclosure until the sun came up, bright and hot, and the children started to complain of hunger. Even then the soldiers would not let us go home or tell us what they wanted with us.

Then an angry soldier came and called out my father's name. My father rose, bowed his head and waited to be shot.

"Come," the angry soldier ordered.

Father said a quick farewell to us and stepped forward. They hurried him away in the direction of Bwana Ruin's house, and we waited to hear the gunshots. We waited a long time. He told us later that he too thought that the day of his death had come.

But that was not the reason the soldiers wanted him. Bwana Ruin was angry that his trusted cook had been rounded up along with the rest of his watu, his people. He had no hot water and no breakfast, and he was very angry.

By the time my father had lit the woodstove, heated the water and cooked breakfast for him, we in the cattle enclosure were cooking under the mid-morning sun. The children cried from hunger. The parents grumbled. No one had the courage to complain to the soldiers guarding us. They stood with their guns pointed at our heads while they smoked cigarettes, ate chocolate and drank Coca-Cola.

Bwana Ruin came at noon. He was a big man, bigger than any man in our village. He was dressed in his usual light green khaki and riding boots. He carried his riding whip wherever he went, even when he did not have the horse, and would sometimes use it to beat up workers who did not take off their hats when he passed by them.

He climbed on the auctioneer's platform and

addressed the workers. His voice was loud and more frightening than his whip when he was angry.

"*Watu*," he said, tapping on the side of his boot with the riding crop. "You know me well. I'm a reasonable bwana, *aye*? *Kweli ama rongo*? True or false, *aye*?"

"*Kweli*," the people said. We knew that other bwanas' watu lived much harder lives.

"When you steal milk from my dairy, do I send you to jail as they would, *aye*?" he asked us. "No, I do not. *Kweli rongo*?"

"*Kweli*," the people said. Bwana Ruin whipped the hide off the culprits instead, and made them pay for the milk.

"When you stole my wheat last year, did I call the police on you, *aye*?" he asked.

He had whipped the thieves senseless and let them go. Everyone knew the men would never steal from him again after the beating they had received.

"When your *totos* steal fruit from my *shamba*," he said, tapping at his boot. "When your children break into my orchard and take my fruit, do I set my dogs on them any more as other bwanas would, *aye*? No, I never do that. I send them to you to discipline yourselves. *Kweli rongo*?"

"*Kweli*," the parents agreed.

He had set his dogs loose on us only once, with tragic results. Now he contented himself with whipping our bare buttocks raw with his riding crop, and then sending us to be properly thrashed by our parents. That did not stop us going back to his orchard. It was the only fruit garden around.

"You know me well, *aye*?" he said. "I am the fairest bwana in the whole of Nanyuki, *aye*? But this time you have gone too far."

He struck at his boot so loud that those children who had fallen asleep woke up, startled.

Bwana Jack Ruin was a big man. He was taller than anyone I knew. Even taller than our headmaster, Lesson One, who we feared like death. Lesson One was so tall that he had to bend forward to enter our classrooms. But Bwana Ruin was taller and stronger. They said that he had once lifted the foreman, the largest worker on the farm, and thrown him right through the dairy — in at one door and out at the other — without touching the floor.

Bwana Ruin was from England. His hair was the color of wheat just before the harvest. He had dark brown spots on his fierce face and on his big hairy arms right down to his fingers. He had a thick wild moustache and hard eyes as green as a cat's. When he was angry, as he was now, his eyes glinted and sparkled and made everyone afraid.

He shook and roared with fury. He waved his fist and brandished his whip at us. Finally he stabbed an angry finger into our midst and swore that no one, not one of us, would leave the cattle pen before his rifle had been returned.

The people looked at one another and wondered who might have done this terrible deed. Bwana Ruin waited for someone to step forward and confess. Standing on the platform high above our heads, he appeared to be the voice and the power of God. No one could defy his might. His all-seeing eyes would show him who the thief was. Then there would be hell to pay. I was a little angry myself when no one came forward to return the stolen gun.

I was twelve years old. I no more understood the frightful things that were going on in the country at large than I understood the things Bwana Ruin said. But the manner in which he spoke and the presence of the angry white soldiers left no doubt in my mind that something more serious than the theft of a single rifle had happened.

The soldiers had set up a big interrogation tent on the other side of the dairy, where they now took the men one by one for questioning. They were gone for a long time. When the men came back, they looked older and crushed. One by one they went, and one by one they came back, all quiet and afraid and unwilling to talk to anyone about it.

We sat in the cattle pen until sunset. We were not allowed to eat or to go to the toilet. Children cried themselves hoarse from hunger and thirst. Women fainted and their men grumbled. They talked and wondered what they should do.

Who could have taken the white man's rifle? Was he going to let their wives and children die for the sake of a gun?

But no one knew anything of the disappeared rifle. Nor of the people called mau-mau, who he said were out to rob and murder and cause chaos throughout the land.

I turned to Hari and asked him in a whisper, "What is mau-mau?"

He kicked me into silence. I did not know it at the time, but mau-mau were the same people we quietly referred to, in whispers, as *andu a mutitu*, the people of the forest. They sometimes came to our house late at night to eat and to talk to Hari in whispers. But I was not allowed to tell anyone about it.

At six o'clock the soldiers allowed us to go back home. They took away nine young men for further questioning. We never saw them again. We heard later that they had been taken for detention to faraway Manda Island. Still later, we heard that they had all died from malaria.

Apart from my father the cook, the houseboy, the herdsmen and the milkmen, no one had done any work that day. No one would get any pay that month. We all missed school that day too. But we got our pay all right when we turned up the following day, in uniform and on time.

The headmaster called us to his office, lined us up against the wall just like the soldiers had lined up the nine young men they had taken away, and demanded to know why we had missed school.

We called the headmaster Lesson One behind his

back. The rest of the time we called him sir. He was a famous terror with his cane and we dared not lie to him. We told him about the raid.

"So?" the headmaster said. "So the soldiers came to your village too?"

"Yes, sir!" we said in unison.

"Then?" he asked us. "Then what happened?"

We went through the whole terrible story once again, adding any little detail we considered sympathetic to our case, all of us talking at the same time. We told him how we had woken up in the night to find our doors broken down and angry white soldiers pointing their guns at our heads. How they had taken us out and threatened to shoot our fathers. We told him how we had spent the whole day in the cattle enclosure without food or water. We told him how the soldiers had taken away nine young men to shoot them dead. We told him everything.

When we had finished talking, the headmaster stopped nodding and asked us, "Then?"

That was when I realized we were in big trouble. The others realized it too, because they were suddenly all very quiet, holding their breath.

"Did the soldiers arrest you?" the headmaster asked.

"No, sir," we answered.

"Then?" he said.

I seriously considered jumping through the window and never coming back to school ever again. But where would I go? My father would tie me up and send my body back to school as usual, in uniform and on time.

He had never been to school himself. He could neither read nor write. But he valued school in a way I would never understand. He often told me in his quiet, subdued way that he did not want me to grow up to be a farm donkey like himself.

Whack! The headmaster's cane came down on the desk so hard that we all jumped with fear.

"Lesson one!" he told us. "There was a raid here in Majengo too yesterday. But the Majengo boys came to school as usual, in uniform and on time."

Whack! Down came the cane on the desk.

"There was a raid at Bwana Hooks' farm too yesterday," the headmaster informed us. "Yet his boys came to school as usual, in uniform and on time."

Whack! came the cane again. A frightened boy wet himself loudly.

"*Bado*," the headmaster told him. "Not yet."

"Lesson one," he said to us. "There was a raid at Bwana Koro's farm yesterday as well. But his boys came to school as usual, in uniform and on time. Now then?"

He smiled at us and said, "Now, tell me again why you did not come to school yesterday."

No one dared. We looked down at our bare feet and waited for doomsday. He gave us time to consider our sin.

"Now then," he said finally. "Do I take it you had no real reason not to come to school yesterday?"

"Yes, sir," we said.

"That you did not come to school yesterday as usual simply because you are lazy, stupid boys?"

"Yes, sir," we agreed.

"Louder!" he ordered.

"Yes, sir," we shouted.

"Now then," he said, smiling in a fatherly way. "You have admitted that you are all sinners. Do you know the wages of sin?"

"Yes, sir." We all knew it.

"What are the wages of sin?" he asked us.

"Death," we told him.

"Again!" he ordered.

"Death," we screamed.

"Louder!"

"Death!"

"Good," he said. "Now you will all face the wall, drop your shorts and bend over for your wages."

He gave us four strokes of the cane each. We had to count the wages of our sin out loud as we received them. It was exactly like death.

Afterwards we stood before him, numb from head to toe with the shock and the pain, unable to think and unable to even shed the tears in our heart. And while pain ran up and down our backsides, the headmaster recited his famous creed.

"Lesson one," he started.

Whack! went the cane.

"It does not matter if you are raided by an army of

soldiers or an army of buffalos," he told us. "You come to school as usual, in uniform and on…?"

"Time!" we yelled.

"Lesson one!"

Whack! The cane again.

"It does not matter if your father's hut catches fire and burns to the ground with your books in it," he told us. "You come to school as usual, in uniform and on…?"

"Time!" we yelled.

"Again!"

"Time!"

"Always on…?"

"Time!"

"Because time is…?"

"Money!"

"Good," he told us. "Lesson one."

Whack!

"It does not matter if you are ill with a cold, stomach worms or diarrhea," he said to us. "You come to school as usual, in uniform and on…?"

"Time!" we yelled.

"And the only time I will excuse you from coming to school is if you are…?"

"Dead!" we yelled.

"Good," he said. "You may go to your classes."

And we rushed out of his office to our classrooms to face the class teachers.

Life at school was one long battle. But there was not much going on in class that day. It was closing day, and the teachers were just as weary of school as we were. They left us to clean the classrooms and prepare them for when we came back after the holidays.

Closing day was also the day the boys settled old scores. The biggest group of boys was from Majengo, the sprawling slum village to which our school was attached. It was made up of the toughest orphans and street urchins and was the most feared. Every farm around Nanyuki had its own gang of rough boys, banding together to protect themselves and each other from the rest.

All the term's quarrels were settled on closing day. That way there was no headmaster to report to, and all would be forgotten by the time school reopened for the next term. The various groups would waylay one another on the way from school and battle it out for hours.

I did not belong to any of these gangs. I did not know how to fight without being hurt or hurting someone. If I hurt someone, and my father found out, he would hurt me worse himself. I dared not win and I could not afford to lose.

But that did not mean I did not get into trouble. From time to time the boys from one gang or the other would gang up and beat the hell out of me just for the fun of it. From time to time too, I would corner the weakest of them and rub his face in the dirt. Then it would start all over again, with me being warned to watch out for closing day.

When closing time came, I left school with a group of

boys from Koro's farm, hiding out in their midst while the boys from Majengo looked all over for me. The boys from Koro's were well known for their fierceness, but they traveled such a long distance to school and back that they had less time to get into fights.

Two

WHEN WE CAME to the log bridge over the river, I said goodbye to the boys from Koro's farm.

The farm was far out in the Loldaiga plain, another five miles away. They had to cross both the Nanyuki and the Liki to get home. I had often chased hares and hunted for warthogs on the grass plateau between the two rivers and on the Loldaiga plain, but I had never been to Koro's farm.

Swinging my school bag over my shoulder, I walked along the river bank toward home. It was dark and lonely along the fishermen's path. The sun never penetrated the old mokoe trees that grew thickly along the river.

But I was not scared. I had walked the forest paths many times before. Alone, I had explored all the forests and caves around Bwana Ruin's farm, and I had never come across anything that frightened me even a little.

I knew the forest very well. On weekends and school holidays I spent a lot of time walking the path between the log bridge and the fish pool near where the farm laborers drew their water. It was peaceful among the cool, dappled shadows, the black river rocks and their cold mountain waters with pools so deep and silent you couldn't hear the water run.

I knew pools where fish jumped all day. I knew hollows under the river banks and the roots of the mokoe trees where wild ducks laid their eggs. I knew caves too cold and dark for ghosts to hide in.

My best secret was the pool where the ducks hid their eggs. I dared not take any of my village friends to these places. I was afraid they would throw stones at the birds or steal their eggs.

I was never in a hurry to get home from school. My mother had an endless list of things to keep a boy busy. The list kept growing, and the only way I knew to keep away from it was to get home late.

"Kariuki," she would say. "Go do this and that. And when you are back, do this and that. Then go down to the river to fetch some water. Then run behind Muturi's hut and fetch me some spinach. Then…"

Before I got back from any of it she would be waiting for me to cut wood for her.

I walked slowly along the river bank, stopping every now and then to watch the red-billed hornbills that feasted on the seeds of the pondo trees. The forest was quiet and peaceful, the silence broken only by the sounds of the birds and the chatter of the monkeys in the trees.

When I came to the duck pool, I hid my bag by the footpath and slid down the steep bank to the river.

Hopping from stone to stone, I came to a sheltered place under the bank. I sat down on a huge rock, dangled my bare feet in the still pool and waited.

If I was still enough, the ducks would come out of their hollows to swim in the pool and to catch insects for their young. Sometimes they would bring their newly hatched ducklings out for me to see.

No one could see me from the path above. Across the river the forest was thick, dark and quiet. It was so dark that crickets could not tell day from night and shrieked all day long.

I sat there for a long while. From time to time a leaf or a seed fell from the trees into the pool, sending beautiful rings eddying across the still water. Occasionally a fish rose to gobble up an insect and then sank back to the bottom of the pool. I knew from experience that they were very hard to catch.

Eventually my patience was rewarded. A family of ducks came floating downstream, moving with the current and letting the water carry them around the rocks and under the roots of the trees. They shot into the still pool and went round and round in the eddies without moving their feet until they reached the dark, quiet places where the water never moved.

There were ten of them — a mother, a father and eight ducklings with yellow bellies and pink feet and beaks. They swam around the pool picking insects and bits of leaves out of the water. The ducklings followed their mother wherever she went, picked at whatever she picked at. She behaved just like a mother hen. The only difference was that she could swim and lived in water.

They were not at all surprised to find me at their favorite pool. We had met many times before and they knew me.

A long green snake shot across the pool, swam very fast past the ducks and slithered into the undergrowth on the far bank. The ducks ignored the snake. I was not afraid either. It was a harmless river snake. I was only afraid of the poisonous puff-adder and the grass vipers.

In the trees above the pool, parrots feasted on the seeds of the pondo trees. A turaco flew down from the tree and went chattering down the river.

Suddenly the father duck squawked and took off downstream, closely followed by the mother duck and her ducklings. In a moment they were gone, ducking under the overhanging bush and out of sight.

I searched the river bank above and along the foot path for the cause of their alarm. Apart from the wind blowing in the trees and the river murmuring on the stones, the forest was quiet.

Then I heard it, the crack of a breaking twig deep in the shadows. I saw a slight movement where the sound had come from.

I peered across the river. For a long moment I saw nothing. Then I saw a dark shadow cross a spot of light. I couldn't tell whether it was human or animal, so faint was the movement.

I sniffed the air. There was the unmistakable smell of

wild buffalo in the air. This made me even more restless. A few weeks before his hunting rifle went missing, Bwana Ruin had shot a lone buffalo that had frightened the herdsmen and killed some dogs in the forest.

I would never forget the smell of buffalo.

I was so busy searching the shadows for buffalo that I did not see the men until they stepped out of the shadows onto the bank. There were two of them, big and bearded, wearing dark green greatcoats. One of them had a big hunting rifle like the one Bwana Ruin had lost, and the other one was armed with a spear and a club.

The one with the gun waved.

I waved back. They did not look like forest guards so I decided to go home. I stood up, fear gnawing at my courage.

"Are you from this farm?" the man asked.

"Yes," I said.

"Do you know Hari?" he asked.

"Yes," I answered.

The men looked at each other. The one with the gun beckoned.

"Come," he said.

"What for?" I asked.

"I want to send you," he said. "To Hari."

He reached into the pocket of his greatcoat. I was quite scared now.

"No," I said. "Don't send me. I must go home now."

"Wait!" he said.

But I could not wait any longer. I hopped back to the

edge of the river and scrambled up the bank. There I came face to face with real terror. Barring my way to the top were three wild men who smelled like buffalo and carried spears and rungus. One of them had a long ugly scar on his cheek.

I dodged past them. The one with the scar caught me by the neck and lifted me off my feet. He shook me like a jimi shaking rabbits in its teeth.

When he put me down I had no more fight left. He held me by the neck until the other two had crossed the river.

"Why do you run?" asked the one with the rifle.

"I want to go home," I wailed.

He studied me for a long moment. I was afraid he would order the other man to fling me into the river.

"Do you know who we are?"

"Let me go!"

"Don't be afraid," he told me. "We are your friends."

They were not. They stole sheep and killed people. That was what everyone said. We were to report when we saw them.

"If you tell the soldiers about us they will come and kill us," he said, "and you will not have friends in the forest anymore. You wouldn't like that, would you?"

There were more of them in the forest. I could not see them but I could smell them, and I heard them breathe.

"Bwana Ruin is a liar," he told me. "All farmers are liars."

It was something I had not thought about. I had been taught to believe that grownups didn't lie.

"I want to send you," the man told me.

Then, taking an envelope from his pocket, he said, "Take this to Hari. And don't show it to anyone else."

He folded it neatly and slipped it in the breast pocket of my shirt. He buttoned up the pocket himself, saying, "If you show it to anyone else I will know."

"Then we will come and get you," said the one with the scar. "And get your mother and your father. Get your brother and sister too."

"I have no sisters."

"We'll get them too," he said.

"I won't show it to anyone," I promised.

"And you must not tell anyone about us."

"I won't."

"Not even your best friend."

"Not even my best friend."

The one with the scar exerted pressure on my neck. It was beginning to hurt.

"We'll cut out your tongue," he said. "How would you like that?"

"Not," I said.

"Good," said the one with the gun. "Don't forget we are watching you."

I lingered only long enough to find my school bag in the bush where I had hidden it. Then I did not stop running until I got out of the forest.

Three

THE RIVER ENTERED Bwana Ruin's farm from the east, in a more or less direct course from the mountains to the grasslands in the west. The laborers' village was the first thing it touched. Then, glancing right, the river flowed past Bwana Ruin's vast orchards and carried on into the plain.

The village consisted of several dozen round mud and thatch huts flung over ten acres of banana trees and vegetable gardens. It was an old village, turned into a maze of winding footpaths among old huts, grain stores and broken latrines. Strangers easily got lost there. Bwana Ruin often promised to demolish it.

My mother's hut was on the far side of the village, close to Bwana Ruin's farmhouse, where he lived alone with his old wife.

I rushed home to find Hari and give him the letter from the people of the forest. As I came up to my mother's hut, she came out with a bucket, thrust it in my hands and ordered me to go down to the river to fetch water.

"Where is Hari?" I asked her.

Hari was still at work, she told me. I had forgotten it was a working day and Hari would be at the dairy skimming Bwana Ruin's milk.

"I have a letter for him," I said.

"A letter? A letter from where?"

I hesitated.

"Give it to me," she said. "I'll give it to Hari when he comes home."

"I can't," I said. "They said I must not talk to anyone about it."

"Who said?" she asked.

"The people who gave it to me."

"Which people?"

I thought about it. Surely "anyone" could not possibly include my own mother. After all, she gave them food when they came to our door at night.

"Give it to me," she said. "I'll keep it for him."

"No," I said, deciding to play it safe. "I'll give it to him myself."

"You go fetch the water," she said, taking my school bag. "After that I want you to chop some firewood."

That was the way it was. Chore after chore after chore. I preferred the peace and the solitude of the duck pool.

I took the bucket and ran behind the hut to the path that led to the river. If I ran fast enough I might be able to chop the wood and still catch Hari at the dairy.

The villagers fetched their domestic water a hundred

yards down the river where the water was dammed with driftwood, forming a deep, dark pool. You stood on the stones by the edge of the pool and immersed your bucket or water gourds without getting your feet wet. Often women took their utensils to the river to wash, so the fish in the dam were well fed and very big. Bwana Ruin fished there for trout. When he was fishing we were not allowed to disturb him and were forced to go elsewhere for our water.

Bwana Ruin was not around. Instead a strange white boy was fishing. He was about my height and build and had hair the color of straw. He was dressed in gray shorts and a jacket and wore hard leather boots like Bwana Ruin's and green knee-high socks.

"Hallo," the boy called out cheerfully.

"Hallo," I said, looking out for Bwana Ruin.

Bwana Ruin was nowhere about. The white boy was fishing with Bwana Ruin's rod, which was twice as long as he was, and he had trouble keeping the line under control. Nevertheless, he had caught one big fish and two small ones, and he called me over to show them to me.

"Lovely, aren't they?" he said proudly.

I had seen bigger catches by Bwana Ruin, but I nodded and said something friendly. Close up the boy was a little shorter than I was, and he had round, red cheeks. His eyes were bright.

"Not bad, is it?" he asked. "I bet you couldn't catch anything as good."

"No," I said. "What's your name?"

"Nigel," he said. "What's yours?"

Just then he felt a nibble on the bait and forgot about me. He gripped the rod with both hands, nervously jerking it back and forth.

"Wait," I said. "Let it swallow the bait."

But he was so excited he hardly heard me. He yanked the rod. The hook shot out of the water without the fish, whipped dangerously over our heads and flew into the mokoe tree above us.

There it rested in the gnarled old branches.

"Oh, dear," said the boy.

He tugged hard on the rod. The hook bit deeper into the tree and the line became hopelessly entangled in the branches. He yanked impatiently on the line. It was obvious that he had not done much fishing before today.

"Wait," I told him. "You will break the line that way. Let me show you."

He gave me the rod. I braced myself as I had seen Bwana Ruin do and tugged gently. I swung the rod this way and that, varying the pressure and direction. But the boy had made a complete mess of it by now and the hook was embedded in a branch fifteen feet above our heads.

There was only one way to get it down.

"Hold here." I handed him back the rod. "I'll climb the tree."

"Good idea," he said.

I spat into my palms and rubbed them together to make them stronger, the way men did before tackling impossible tasks. Then I hugged the tree trunk with my legs and arms and started to climb.

I had been climbing trees as long as I could remember and I had no difficulty at all getting to the branch where the hook was stuck. I released the line and threw the hook down. Then I looked around.

I had never been up this particular tree and was surprised at the view. I could see all the way over the orchards to Bwana Ruin's house. Father was in the kitchen garden picking tomatoes. Mamsab Ruin sat on the veranda reading a book while Salt and Pepper, Bwana Ruin's very fierce dogs, lay by the door sunning themselves. Outside the dairy, past Bwana Ruin's house, a line of children waited to receive their daily ration of skimmed milk. Far out on the plains was the airstrip, the black-and-white wind sock moving lazily in the wind.

The tree I sat in was thick with hooks. There were dozens of beautifully feathered hooks, a tribute to Bwana Ruin's impatience, and numerous crude ones made from safety pins, which the villagers lost when they went poaching at night. I decided to leave them all where they were until I could come back alone and fetch them. They would fetch me a good price from the village boys who were great fishermen, even though it was strictly forbidden.

The branch where I sat was heavy with fruit. I picked a few of the deep purple fruit and ate one. It was rough to the tongue but very sweet, so I decided to stay on the tree and have some more.

"What are you eating?" the white boy asked.

"Fruit," I told him. "Have some."

I threw him a few. He tasted one, spat it out and threw the rest into the river. Then he went back to fishing.

I was disappointed. I had expected the white boy to love the taste of wild fruit like any other boy. Then I remembered he had a whole orchard of exotic fruit to pick from.

I crawled farther on, eating my way along the branch overhanging the pool.

"Do you like to fish?" he asked me.

"Very much," I said.

"Would you like to catch one?"

"No," I told him. "Fishing is not allowed."

Bwana Ruin mercilessly whipped any boy caught fishing in his river. The white boy could not understand how the river belonged to Bwana Ruin, so I explained it to him.

"This farm belongs to Bwana Ruin," I told him. "Don't you know that?"

He knew who owned the farm but not the river.

"The river also," I told him. "Everything belongs to Bwana Ruin."

I told him how, just the week before, the forest guards had caught some boys fishing and handed them over to Bwana Ruin. Bwana Ruin had whipped the boys raw and threatened to fire their fathers.

My father would kill me if I ever lost him his job.

Where he came from, the white boy told me, the rivers were for everyone. Anyone could fish anywhere, anytime.

"Where do you come from?" I asked.

He told me he came from Yorkshire.

"Where is that?" I asked.

"England."

I knew England. Everything we used was made in England. From the pencils and the rubbers we used in school to the hoes we used in the gardens. They were all made in England. The first English words I had learned to read were Made in England. But I had no idea where England was and suggested we might go fishing there one day.

Nigel laughed.

"We can't. It's a long way from here."

"Farther than the Loldaiga hills?" I asked, pointing at the blue hills on the horizon.

"Farther," he said.

"Farther than the place where the earth meets the sky?" I asked.

"Farther," he said. "You can't walk there."

"How did you come here then?"

"I came by air," he said. "I came in an airplane."

"You have an airplane?"

I would not have been at all surprised if he had an airplane. To many of us village children, white people were strange creatures who were allowed many impossibilities. Many white farmers in Laikipia owned private planes and private airstrips. Bwana Ruin himself owned an airstrip, and sometimes white people came by plane to see him.

But no, the white boy had not come in his own airplane. He had come in an airliner. A big, big plane that belonged to the government.

"Where is it?" I asked.

"It's in Nairobi," he told me.

I knew Nairobi from my books in school, but it was the first time I had met someone who had ever been there. I felt foolish and ignorant in front of this white boy.

"Have you ever caught a warthog?" I asked.

"A warthog? What's that?"

Now we were even as far as airplanes and warthogs went.

"It's a very big animal," I told him.

I had never caught a warthog either, though I had hunted them. But I did not tell him this.

His parents were back in England, he told me. He had come to stay with his grandparents for the summer holidays. Up until then, I had assumed he had come to the farm with a visiting family. It took me a moment to understand that by grandparents he meant Bwana and Mamsab Ruin.

"In that case," I said, "we can't go hunting together. Bwana Ruin is very *kali*, very fierce."

At that moment he got another bite on the bait, and we forgot about Bwana Ruin. Again he was too hasty in whipping the line out of the water, and it ended up in the tree next to where I lay. I released it and dropped it back into the river.

"I think I had better stay up here," I said, "until you finish." So I crawled along the branch and ate some more fruit.

Then my mother showed up. She had the habit of turning up suddenly whenever I started to forget my chores, and this time I had completely forgotten about the water I had come to fetch for her.

She stormed down to the river bank calling my name. I did not know whether to jump into the river or remain where I was. I feared her tongue-lashing as much as I dreaded my father's whip.

I remained where I was.

She found the bucket on the bank and stopped. She looked uncertainly from the bucket to the river, no doubt wondering if I had drowned. I lay in the tree hoping she would take the bucket and go home, leave me to explain later.

She was about to do exactly that when the white boy spoiled it all.

"Hallo," he said. "Are you looking for something?"

My mother did not understand a word of English. She had no idea the white boy was talking to her. Then he looked up the tree and asked me, "What does she want?"

I kept very still. My mother followed his eyes up the tree and discovered me where I was, doing my best to become invisible.

"What are you doing in the tree?" she asked me.

"Nothing."

"Come down from there at once," she ordered.

In all the time I had been up that tree, I had not for a moment stopped to think how I would eventually get back on the ground. I was lying on a huge, thick branch, facing away from the trunk. There was no room to turn around, and moving backwards was just as impossible.

"Did you hear me?" my mother shouted. "I said come down here now."

I rushed to obey. Halfway through the maneuver, I slipped and went crashing through the branches into the pool. Cold, dark water engulfed me.

As I went under, I heard Nigel call out. I had never been in water higher than my waist, and I yelled out in fear. My mother could not swim either and I would certainly have drowned if it had not been for the white boy. Nigel jumped in clothes and all and dragged me out of the pool.

As I clambered onto the bank, gasping for air and spitting out water, my mother pulled me up and gave me a thorough shaking.

"What happened to the water I sent you to fetch?" she demanded.

Before I could answer, she thrust the bucket in my hands and said, "I want you home with the water before I get there."

Then she turned and stormed away.

I had no time to thank the white boy. I grabbed the

bucket, dipped it into the river and rushed after my mother. By the time she got home, I was right there behind her, panting and shivering from the cold.

"Get the firewood!" she ordered.

I ran behind the hut. She had chopped the wood herself, after waiting for nearly an hour, and all I had to do was bring it in and arrange it neatly by the fireplace. That was quickly done.

"Anything else?" I asked eagerly.

"Why?" she asked. "Where do you want to go?"

"Nowhere," I said.

When she did not mention any other chore, I sneaked out of the hut and ran back to the river.

Halfway there I ran into my father.

"You," he barked.

I stopped so suddenly I almost fell over him. He was dressed in his cook's uniform — white trousers, a white vest and a green apron. On his head, like a huge white pot, was the cook's hat.

"Where are you going?" he asked me.

"To the river," I said.

"To the river?" he said loudly. "To do what at the river?"

"Nothing."

I had learned, the hard way, that the right reply was not always the safest reply. But I was not allowed to lie. So "nothing," "nowhere" and "I don't know" were my safest replies.

"You are wet," he said scoldingly.

"I fell in the river."

He rapped me on the head with his knuckles, a practice I found painful and insulting.

"Didn't I tell you not to go fishing?" he asked me.

"I didn't go fishing," I told him. "I went to fetch water."

"Are you lying to me?" he asked.

"No, Father," I said.

He seemed to believe me. He lifted his tall hat and took a paper bag from under it.

"Take this to your mother," he said, giving it to me. "Run."

I ran like a rabbit. After taking the package home, I followed a different route down to the fishermen's path and back to the pool.

It was nearly dark now and the white boy had called it a day. He had caught a second big fish and was hooking it on a forked stick to carry home. He hooked the two small fish on another forked stick and gave it to me.

"Take these," he said.

"Take them where?" I asked.

"To your cook," he said.

My cook? I did not have a cook, I told him. My mother did all the cooking and she hated fish. I was not even supposed to eat fish.

"But it is good fish," he told me.

I wanted to be his friend, I told him, but I could not accept the fish. They would skin me alive if I did.

"Who would skin you alive?" he wanted to know.

"Everyone," I told him. My father, my mother, my brother Hari, the whole lot of them. And Bwana Ruin too, if he ever found out I had eaten his fish.

"Tell them I gave you the fish," the white boy told me. "Here, take it. Go on, it's yours."

There was no arguing with him. He didn't know what a terror the life of a village boy was. I was not supposed to see anything, hear anything, say anything or do anything without first asking permission from the grownups.

I accepted the stick of fish to make him happy, and we walked together along the path from the river.

"How do you eat it?" I asked him.

The white boy turned to me, surprised.

"Have you never eaten fish before?" he asked.

My experience with fish stopped at catching it. One day Hari had caught, cooked and eaten a whole trout by himself. He would not let me have any, because he said it had sharp bones that were dangerous if swallowed.

"You eat it like chicken," the white boy told me. "Like chicken."

"What about the bones?" I asked.

"Your cook will take them out for you."

My mother knew even less than I did about eating fish. The smell of it made her want to throw up. After Hari had cooked his fish, she had made me clean her pots for two days before she would use them again.

"What's your name?" the white boy asked, when we came to the fork in the path. The path to the left led to the farmhouse, while the one on the right led to the village.

"Kariuki."

"Carrookee?" he said. "It was nice meeting you."

We shook hands and he went on his way.

I waited until he was out of sight. Then I swung the fish over my head and hurled them as far as I could into the bush. I was not foolish enough to believe I could convince my father that a strange white boy had given me the fish. Then I turned and froze.

Coming behind me, along the river walk, was Bwana Ruin. He was accompanied by the fierce dogs the whole village dreaded, the Alsatian attack dogs called Salt and Pepper. They had once killed a leopard all by themselves, torn it to pieces between them with their strong teeth. They were trained to attack anyone Bwana Ruin did not like. And Bwana Ruin did not like village children.

The dogs charged up to me. Bwana Ruin barked an order and they stopped and went back to him. I stood frozen with terror as they walked slowly up to me. He was even bigger and more frightening close up. It was rumored that he could see in the dark like a cat.

"*Toto*." He called all village children toto. "What was that you threw away when you saw me coming, *aye*?"

"Nothing, Bwana," I answered.

"Nothing, *aye*?"

"Nothing, *aye*."

He took me by the ear and pinched hard.

The dogs growled at me. They could hardly wait for orders to tear me to pieces.

"Fetch," he ordered.

They said he could also see into people's heads and tell what they were thinking. He was a truly formidable man.

I went into the bush after the fish. And, just in case I thought of running away, the dogs came with me, sniffing at my heels and growling.

It was nearly dark now and it took me a while to find the fish, still on the stick. I brought it back to him.

"Nothing, *aye*?" he said, taking me by the ear again. "Just a spot of poaching, *aye*?"

I was too frightened to utter a word. Bwana Ruin took me by the ear and walked me to the farmhouse. He took me round to the kitchen door and called my father.

My father nearly died when he saw me with the fish.

"Kariuki," he spoke softly, though there was murder in his eyes. "What have you done?"

"Nothing," I told him.

He was about to start rapping my head right away when Bwana Ruin ordered him to ask me if I knew that it was forbidden to fish.

"I'll skin you today, I promise," my father told me instead.

Bwana Ruin did not understand our language.

"But, Father…" I started.

"You want me to lose me my job," he said.

"No, Father."

"*Kira*," he ordered. "Quiet!"

Everything my father said to me was an order. I could not remember ever having a friendly conversation with him.

"How many times have I told you not to fish?" he asked me.

"I don't know," I said.

"How many?" he barked.

"Many times?" I said.

"You never listen, do you?" he asked.

"But, Father…"

"Do you?" he repeated.

"No, Father."

I was expecting a rap on the head with the knuckles, but the slap caught me by surprise. The force of it knocked me into the flower bushes. I lay there pretending to be dead, but he knew my tricks. He hauled me out by the ears and finally gave me a painful rapping on the head with his knuckles.

"Why did you catch fish?" he demanded.

"I did not catch any fish," I cried. "The boy gave it to me. The *mzungu* boy gave it to me."

The next slap left my ears ringing. He was in an enraged mood and would have beaten me senseless if Bwana Ruin had not intervened.

"Enough," said Bwana Ruin. "Call his father here and tell him he is fired."

My father turned gray. The expression on his face was terrifying to see. I had never seen him so angry and confused.

"Bwana!" he said to Bwana Ruin. "This boy is my boy."

"Your boy, *aye*?" Bwana Ruin stopped and came back. "He is your son? Why didn't you tell me that before?"

Father said nothing.

Bwana Ruin looked from me to him and shook his head.

"I have told him not to fish, Bwana," my father said. "I have told him many times not to catch fish. But I will teach him a lesson today. He will never fish again, Bwana. I promise he will never again catch any fish."

Seeing that they would not give me a chance to defend myself, I decided to take the risk and speak up.

"The *mzungu* boy gave me the fish," I said to Bwana Ruin.

"Which *mzungu* boy, *aye*?" he asked me.

"He means the Bwana Kidogo," my father said. "The little master from England."

"Nigel gave you the fish, *aye*?" Bwana Ruin asked me.

"Yes, Bwana," I said.

"Nigel," he called into the house. "Nigel, come here."

While we waited for him, my father rapped me on the head with his knuckles, saying, "You will explain all this when I come home tonight."

Nigel emerged from the house and greeted me again.

"Hallo," he said, smiling. "You haven't taken your fish home?"

Bwana Ruin looked from him to me. "Do you know this native boy?" he asked.

"I met him by the river," Nigel said. "He helped me with my line and fell in the river. That's why he is all wet."

"And you gave him the fish?" Bwana Ruin asked him.

"He didn't want it," Nigel said. "I made him take it. For helping me."

"Go in the house and change," Bwana Ruin said to him.

"Can I go fishing with him tomorrow?" Nigel asked.

"I don't think so," said Bwana Ruin. "We must not encourage the boys to fish. They will poach the rivers dry if we do, won't they? Now come along and change. It's nearly dinnertime."

They went into the house, leaving us standing there together. My father looked devastated.

"Go home," he ordered. "We shall discuss this when I come home."

Halfway back to the village, I realized I was still carrying the stick with the fish. I swung it over my head and hurled it as far into the bush as I could.

Then I ran home to face my mother.

Four

THE FOLLOWING DAY, Nigel came looking for me. He found me up to my neck in the chores my mother had invented just to keep me busy and out of trouble.

"Let's go fishing," he said.

I reminded him of the night before and showed him the bruises I had suffered. He could not understand how all the fish in the river belonged to his grandfather.

"It can't be," he said. "The river is so big."

I had tried reasoning that way once with my father. I could go far upstream or downstream, I had said. Surely one man could not own a whole river and all the fish in it.

That time too, my reasoning had earned me a rapping on the head.

"Let's go swimming," Nigel said.

"I can't swim."

"I'll teach you," he said.

The idea appealed to me. But I still had wood to chop and several other things to do for my mother. He offered to help.

I gave him the ax and showed him the wood to chop. He had never used an ax before. It was a big, heavy ax and I had to show him how to hold it.

The very first chop was a near disaster. He swung the ax at the loose piece of wood. The piece of wood leapt up at him. He ducked. The wood shot past his right eye and nearly killed Hari's dog sleeping on the dust behind us.

The dog yelped and crawled under the grain store.

"Not like that," I said to Nigel. "Like this."

I showed him how to hold the wood down with his foot so it would not snap back and knock his head off. Then I stood back and watched him nearly chop his boot off with the second swing of the ax. He found it all very amusing.

We were having a merry time of it when Hari showed up. He regarded the white boy with surprise and asked me who he was.

"He is my friend," I told him.

I asked him what he was doing back home at this time of day. In reply, he asked me if I had seen anyone on my way from school the day before.

"No," I said.

He took me by the ears and lifted me off my feet. He carried me out of Nigel's hearing.

"Did you see anyone on your way from school yesterday?" he asked again.

"Yes," I said, remembering.

He put me down then. He had a habit of hitting me

whenever I did something he did not like. He had a terrible left and right combination that left my brains fairly scrambled. The left knocked me to the right and the right bounced me back. I complained often about it to my mother, but the most help I ever got was the advice to stay away from Hari. He was a grown-up man now, she told me. He had no time to play with boys.

The worst thing about Hari's beating was not the force itself, which was enough to knock me unconscious. It was knowing that the right slap was coming after the left and there was nothing I could do about it. Once I had made the mistake of ducking and Hari's hand had knocked a hole the size of a boy's head in the mud wall of the hut. That time he had nearly beaten me senseless.

"Did they give you anything for me?" Hari asked.

"Yes," I said.

I was giving the right answers, so the next left-right caught me quite unawares. I was half deaf by now. I heard Hari repeat the question from miles away as he reached into my pocket for the letter the man had put there.

The shirt had been dried overnight by the fireplace, and the letter had dried out with it. It fell apart as Hari opened it, and he looked at me for an explanation.

"I fell in the river," I told him.

He looked from the letter to me. I considered running away — far, far away to the land of the Dorobo — and never coming back.

"Stay still," he warned.

Slowly he unfolded the letter. The ink had run all over it. It looked like a page from one of my school books after the rain caught me halfway between home and school and found the books under my armpit where I carried them to keep them dry. The headmaster had nearly killed me that time too.

The expression on Hari's face warned me to get out of there fast. I stepped back, tripped over the piece of wood the mzungu boy was chopping and went crashing into the dust. Hari kicked me hard and went away very angry.

Nigel was totally amazed by the encounter.

"Who was that?" he asked.

"Hari," I said. "My brother Hari."

"What did he want?"

"Nothing."

"He whacks you like that just for fun?"

"It doesn't hurt much," I said and smiled.

"Can't you report him to your father?" he asked.

The last time I told my father that someone had beaten me up in school, my father had called me a coward and gave me a rapping too. So I went back to school and walloped the bully right back. The bully's mother complained to my mother. She reported it to my father, and I got another beating for that.

I had long given up trying to understand the world of adults.

Nigel could not understand the brutality that dogged the everyday life of a village boy.

"Doesn't your father ever beat you?" I asked him.

"No," he told me. "Never."

"And your mother?" I asked.

She never beat him either.

"What about your big brothers?" I asked him.

He had no brothers.

And the teachers? I asked him. Didn't the teachers whack him all the time?

"Never," he told me.

I could not help envying him. I told him how the life of a village boy was difficult. Everyone beat the fun out of you. There was no hope of peace until you were grown, circumcised and became a man. Then no one would touch you, not even your mother.

The wood-chopping business was getting nowhere. Nigel suggested we give it up and do something less tiring. We could go down and explore the forest along the river.

I called Hari's dog, Jimi. He was lying on the dust under the grain store playing dead. He opened one eye, regarded me for a moment.

With no one else in the compound to talk to, I talked to Jimi a lot. I asked him if he would like to go for a walk.

He turned the other way as if to say, "Leave me alone."

"I have a good idea," I said to him.

He did not want to hear it. He was fed up with my bright ideas. Some of them had nearly got him killed.

I grabbed him by the neck and hauled him out from

under the grain store. He was my dog, or at least Hari let me call him my dog, and he had to do as I commanded.

Everything in our village ran according to a hierarchy. Above everyone were Bwana Ruin, Mamsab Ruin and any white person who happened to come along. Then came the village men. Then came the women and girls. And then came the rest of us. The boys and village dogs were at the bottom of the ladder, below the goats, the sheep and the chickens. We boys had no rights whatsoever. Not at home, not in the village and not at school.

But the dogs were in a worse situation. We, at least, had names we could call our own. The dogs had none. No one wasted time worrying about what to name his dog. Every other dog in the village was simply called Dog. The rest were named Jimi. It was not strange at all for a person to have three dogs named Jimi. This confused the dogs more than it confused the boys, the village dog handlers.

However, in the presence of other dogs, only Hari's jimi answered to the name Jimi. He was a true mongrel like the rest of them, a strange crossbreed of all the dogs that had ever lived. He was bigger and meaner than the rest and was the leader of all the village dogs. He was also one of the oldest dogs in the village and was father and grandfather to most of the other mongrels.

I nudged Jimi with my foot.

"Let's go chase rabbits," I said to him. "You are growing fat and lazy and ugly."

He rose, walked a few paces farther under the grain store and lay down again to sleep. Once, when he was weak and dying from hunger and fleas, Jimi had been my dog and best friend. But as he grew bigger and stronger, Hari had reclaimed him and promised to find me another starved, flea-bitten puppy to love. Jimi owed me his life, and I never missed an opportunity to remind him of it.

"Leave him be," I said to Nigel. "We'll take the other jimis."

I whistled for Hari's other dogs. I never took them anywhere if I could help it, so they eagerly rose to go with me. When Jimi saw that we really intended to leave him out of the adventure, he got up, shook the dust from his fur and took his place by my side.

We made our way through the village paths. I led us away from any route where we might come upon my father or mother. We were joined by numerous other jimis along the way, dogs that had nothing better to do than tag along with us. We joined the fishermen's path and went up the river, away from the village and the farmhouse.

Nigel had never been in a forest this big and wild before. Everything was new and wonderful to him. He was amazed by the things he saw. The trees, the birds and the insects were all new to him. It was soon clear to me that he knew as little about my world as I knew about his.

Nigel ran about with the dogs, swung from the liana

and leaped over the rocks. He roared like a fearsome giant and flexed his thin muscles. He leaped into the river, clothes and all, and wrestled with giant crocodiles. That was the first day he told me about Tarzan. He wanted to grow up to be Tarzan, a fearless giant who lived in the forest and was not afraid of anything.

I knew I was going to like Nigel, this white boy who knew so little about everything. I had a great deal to teach him. But first he had to teach me to swim.

"We have no swimming trunks," he said.

"Swimming trunks?"

"Swimming shorts," he said.

He was surprised to hear that I knew of no such shorts. I owned two pairs of shorts — the ones I wore at home and the ones I wore to school. I swam in the nude, like all the boys I knew.

To show him there was really nothing to it, I undressed and rolled my clothes into a ball. I stuffed them into a hollow under the root of a mokoe tree. I had learned this from Hari. If the river guards showed up when I was in the river, I would run off into the forest and come back for my clothes later.

I jumped into the river. The water came up to my knees and was very cold. Nigel took off his clothes too and joined me in the pool.

We splashed about for a while. The dogs got bored and went off into the forest to look for something to eat. Nigel tried to teach me to float, but the pool was too shallow.

"We'll find another one," I told him. "This river is full of pools."

We dressed and went farther up the river. We could not walk quickly, as Nigel had to see everything, touch everything and smell everything. He asked questions about everything he saw. About the trees and about the birds. About the hundreds of insects and things that lived on the moss-covered trees and in the under-growth. He had nature study in school and had read scores of books and encyclopedias on nature. But he had never seen anything as wonderful as this forest.

I was very proud of my forest.

"Can you read a book?" he asked me.

I told him that I could. I was in class five. He was in class six. I told him about my school. I tried to tell him about our much-feared headmaster, Lesson One, but his mind was on many things.

We came upon a convoy of safari ants crossing our path. Nigel immediately stopped and kneeled by the path to study them. I sat on the bank and told him how the safari ants invaded our village during the long rains, and how we spent sleepless nights fighting them off.

He stuck his finger into their path and withdrew it with a cry as a giant soldier ant sank its teeth into it. He tried a blade of grass and watched the soldier ants attack it furiously. He looked up to ask how one fought off such small creatures.

"First you take off your clothes," I told him. "That way they have nowhere to hide. Then you pick them off your body one at a time and throw them into the fire. After that you hold your clothes over the fire so that the smoke blinds them. Then you burn old bicycle tires to drive them out of the hut."

If you had no old tires, old shoes — especially gum boots — did just as well.

We did not always win. Sometimes we had to move out and leave the ants in charge of the house until they saw it fit to move on.

Nigel's green eyes were full of wonder. He had a broad face, a freckled nose, red cheeks and a happy smile. I had no doubt he could see in the dark too, like Bwana Ruin.

He was getting hungry. He suggested we catch a fish and roast it over a fire.

"We have no fire," I told him.

"Yes, we do," he said.

He always carried a box of matches with him. He was a boy scout, he told me. He was always prepared.

"We have no line," I said reasonably.

"We can use our hands." He had seen Amazon Indians do this in a film.

"I don't know how to eat fish," I confessed.

"I'll show you," he said, and we hopped off the bank into the river.

The fish found in the Liki and Nanyuki rivers were mountain trout. They had many fine bones that could get stuck in a boy's throat and kill him. It was said, mainly by Hari and other poachers, that it cost a hundred shillings at the local hospital to remove a fish bone from your throat. More than twice my father's monthly salary. The fear was deep.

I was later to learn that this rumor was started by Bwana Ruin to discourage the villagers from fishing in his river, and spread by Hari and his kind who had no wish to share their catch with the whole village.

I loved fishing for the sake of fishing. The tingling sensation when a fish nibbled at the bait, the thrill of landing it. I had never fished with my hands and thought it a foolish and impossible task. But Nigel believed in it, and as he was now my friend, I went along with the idea.

We wasted some time that morning trying to catch fish with our bare hands. Finally we had to settle for the purple koe fruit that grew wild all along the river bank. I considered taking Nigel to the duck pool to introduce him to my ducks, but before I could make the suggestion, the dogs came back, making a big noise in the forest. They had been as far as the middle plain, Jimi told me. They had caught and eaten something and some were still licking their lips. They were doing much better than us as far as food was concerned. Nigel suggested we get them to catch something for us.

I explain that jimis did not catch anything for anyone. It was everyone for himself and too bad for the slowest. They ate everything on the spot — first come first served — dividing the catch so fast that only blood and a few hairs remained. The slowest jimis had to be content with licking the blood off the leaves and the grass.

"You have to be fast," I said to Nigel.

"I'm very fast," he told me.

So I called the jimis and gave them the plan. They were all mongrels and many of them were slow to catch on. They gazed at me, bored. They had heard it all before.

I turned to Hari's Jimi and instructed him to keep the others in line. And to make certain that Nigel and I got a share of whatever we caught.

Jimi looked balefully back at me and would have laughed at me if he could. But he understood, all right. He turned his glance across the river and said something encouraging to his followers. Then he rose and splashed across the river and into the trees.

The hunt was on.

Five

WE SPLASHED ACROSS the river after the dogs. Following their loud rustling through the undergrowth, we rushed on into the forest.

The forest grew thicker and darker as we penetrated deeper into the interior. The ground rose steadily as we left the river valley. The forest floor changed from rich, soft soil to hard, rocky ground.

We ran on after the dogs. Nigel's hair caught on the undergrowth, slowing him down. Several times I had to stop and help untangle it.

"Are you tired?" I asked.

"No," he said, hopping with excitement.

"Are you afraid?"

"No."

He had never been in such a place before.

"This is nothing," I told him. "Wait until we get to the Liki."

We pushed on after the dogs. We heard them forcing their way through the bush just ahead of us, searching the forest for rabbits and hares.

Hours later, we emerged from the dense forest onto the middle plateau, a vast grassland between the two rivers. Apart from a few rain clouds over the mountain miles away to the east, the sky was a clear blue dome above us. The rainy season was not due for another three months, and it was a beautiful day to be out hunting, cool and clear, and the air was crisp and fresh.

Across the plain was the Liki valley. It was as thickly forested as the Nanyuki river valley we had just left. But the best hunting ground in all the world was the Loldaiga plain. Old Moses, the largest warthog I had ever seen, lived there.

The ground around us was open to the horizon. We saw the dogs sniffing their way through the grass, searching each and every clump of bush that grew around the scattered cedar trees.

On the bushes grew many kinds of berries. Some of them were poisonous but most of them were good to eat. I showed Nigel which ones were edible.

"Never eat strange berries," I told him. "They can kill you very quickly. You must watch the birds. Don't eat anything they don't eat."

Nigel had read a great deal about jungles, and he knew some of these rules. But everything he had seen so far was bigger, more awesome than anything he had ever read. He told me again about Tarzan. He lived with the animals and was king of the jungle.

I knew the forest around Bwana Ruin's farm well. I also knew all the caves and all the hiding places. But I had never before heard of the white giant. The only king of the jungle I knew was a giant one-eyed ogre with two mouths — one on his face, the other at the back of his head — who lived in caves up on the mountain. He carried a small bag on his shoulder into which he put the children he caught for his dinner.

I was telling Nigel about the giant of the small bag, and about his encounter with Old Moses the warthog, when a big snake cut across our path at a terrific speed.

Nigel grabbed for the snake's tail. I tackled him and threw him to the ground, away from the snake. The snake sped away, pursued by a few foolish jimis who had never seen a giant cobra before and thought it a good snack.

My heart was beating wildly as I helped Nigel back to his feet.

"What did you do that for?" he protested. "I'm not afraid of snakes."

His ignorant daring seemed to have no end.

The dogs mobbed the cobra, yelping and leaping and trying to bite him. The snake suddenly stopped, coiled himself into a spring and, raising his head, dared them to come any nearer. The dogs paused to think about it. They surrounded the snake and waited for the bravest of them to take the first bite at this angry lunch. Jimi, who had survived several snake attacks on this same plain, kept well away.

Finding himself outnumbered by the yelping, slobbering jimis, the cobra slithered into a rabbit hole and stayed put. Some young and foolish jimis started to dig him out.

Some snakes were harmless, I told Nigel. But most were not, and you could not always tell which was which. So if he saw any snake bigger than his little finger, he was to run like a hare.

"But I'm not afraid of snakes," he told me.

Ahead of us, Hari's Jimi gave a surprised yelp as a startled hare, escaping from the cobra, shot out of the emergency exit of his burrow and took off at high speed. The jimis abandoned whatever they were doing and joined in the chase. We ran after them.

The hare ran so fast that he seemed no more than a bouncing ball of fur. Jimi raced after him, leaping and bounding and crashing through everything that stood between him and his prey. The hare seemed to realize he stood no chance in a straight race against Jimi. He started weaving and dodging and zigzagging in and out of clumps of bush. He raced through the tall grass at such a high speed that the pursuing dogs became dizzy from the chase. They tripped and somersaulted, crashed into each other and rolled all over the plain.

The hare led us across the plateau toward the Liki valley. After half a mile the yelping died down and we lost track of the jimis altogether. We ran on, desperate to get to the hare before the jimis had eaten it all up.

When we finally caught up with them, the dogs were sniffing the ground in confusion, unaware that the hare had gone underground. Then Jimi showed them the hole where the hare had vanished. They went mad thinking how to get the hare out. The hole was too narrow for any of them to squeeze into.

Jimi decided the surest way was to burrow into the hole and started digging.

"This could take hours," I said to Jimi as he set to work, tossing the soil in all directions.

Jimi did not mind. He went right on digging, throwing soil and grass back into our eyes. We stepped aside and let him dig.

"What now?" I wondered.

"Fire," Nigel shouted with excitement. "Let's smoke him out."

We gathered twigs and dry grass. We heaped them over the hole. We were getting ready to light the fire when I looked up and saw our hare. He had popped out of an emergency exit about fifty yards away and was watching us and no doubt wondering what in the world we were up to.

"Jimi," I said, the excitement rising inside me. "Look, Jimi. There he is."

Jimi went on digging. The others watched him. Some were bored enough to lie down and doze off.

Then the hare, having apparently decided that this had nothing at all to do with him, turned and went on his way.

"Jimi," I yelled and pointed. "There he goes. Look."

Jimi finally stopped digging and looked up. The jimis also turned to look. By the time they had an idea what I was talking about, the hare was a hundred yards away, bobbing and weaving and going like the wind. Jimi gave a yelp and bounded after him. The other dogs followed.

The hare led us across the plain and straight into the thick forest along the Liki valley. With excited yelping, the dogs crashed into the woods after him.

The forest was too dense for us to push our way through. We crawled on all fours and passed under the first line of thorny undergrowth. We crawled for a hundred yards before we were able to stand and survey our surroundings.

"Can we rest a bit?" Nigel said, panting with the excitement.

His shoes were killing him, he told me. I had never worn shoes myself, so I had no idea what he was going through. We sat on a dead log to rest. We heard the dogs run on and on. The sound of the chase faded until it died away altogether. The forest was all quiet around us.

It took Nigel a while to get his breath. He had never gone on this sort of an expedition before, he told me. Where he came from, there was no running involved in hunting. The hunter sneaked up to a deer and shot him in the head before the deer knew he was there. There was no fun or excitement in it at all. Nothing was as much fun as this.

The yelping of the dogs started again. We heard them change directions several times as the hare led them on a wild tour of the whole forest. They were miles away from us by now. The yelping gradually faded in the distance.

"Have they caught him?" Nigel asked.

"I don't think so," I said.

They had never chased a hare that far or that long before. Maybe they discovered that they had been chasing their own echo all this time. It had happened before.

We listened for a while. With the dogs now silent, the forest around us took on a cold, sinister air. The shadows were deepening and shifting as the sun went over the hills.

I whistled for the dogs. The spooky silence weighed down on us.

"There is nothing to be afraid of here," I said, as much to myself as to Nigel. "I have been in the forest many times on my own."

"Really?"

"With the jimis," I told him.

We sat and waited for the dogs to return. The shadows turned to darkness and the cold chill of the Liki crept up the valley and through the forest toward us.

"It's getting dark," Nigel observed.

It was time to go home.

"What about the dogs?" he asked.

"They know their way home," I told him.

He pulled on his shoes and we prepared to leave.

Then we heard a sudden yelp from not far away. We froze. The terrified yelp was followed by a crashing sound much like the noise of a falling tree. The crashing noise, however, went on and on. Instead of fading away, the sound grew louder. The jimis joined in the chase, their yelping chorus echoing through the forest.

When Nigel spoke, his voice trembled.

"What's that?" he asked.

I had no idea. He edged closer to me. I was quite frightened myself, but I dared not show it.

We waited with bated breath, uncertain which way to run.

The continuous crashing sound grew louder and louder. It swept like an angry storm through the forest. We clung to the log where we sat and listened as the dogs bayed and yelped after whatever it was that they were driving toward us. We were really scared now.

With a deafening roar, the sound burst upon us — a shocking wave of blurry, black fury that knocked us off our log with the force of its passage. The thing barely glanced at us, its dilated nostrils spewing steaming breath, the terrifying red eyes burning with rage. Then it turned away, stepped back into the blackness and was gone.

"Wow!" Nigel was totally amazed. "What was that?"

"Buffalo," I told him.

He was shaking now, and I was breathless with fear.

The dogs shot past us, running like the wind after the disappearing disaster. Nigel leaped to his feet and went after them. I ran after him. He blustered through the darkening forest, oblivious to the thorns and things that clutched at his clothes and tore at his hair.

By the time I caught up with him, the chase was miles away from us and fading. I took his hand and ran in a different direction, led him away from the direction the dogs had taken.

"Where are you going?" he yelled at me.

"Home," I yelled back.

"Are we not going after them?" he asked.

"No," I said, still running with him.

"What if they catch the buffalo?"

"Jimis don't catch buffalo," I said. "Jimis can't catch buffalo. Buffalo kills jimis. Buffalo kills people too."

"Why are they chasing him, then?" he asked.

My guess was that the jimis had not actually seen their quarry yet. That they were chasing the fury and the thunder and had no idea what they were running after.

We ran on. We cut across the forest at an angle to emerge from the valley as far away from the buffalo's path as possible. We were out of breath when we climbed the last rise onto the grass plateau. Far away to the left we could hear the dogs in full cry after their prey. Only then did we stop running.

Nigel was worried about the dogs. I told him to think of us instead. We were miles from home and it was getting dark.

But he came from a land where dogs mattered more than people, it seemed.

"Don't worry about the jimis," I told him. Jimis were survivors. I had never known of a jimi to be killed on a hunting expedition. On the other hand, I knew of scores of boys who had been seriously gored by a rampaging buffalo. But these facts did not interest Nigel.

"How will they find their way home?" he asked.

His concern for the dogs amazed me. So did his endless ignorance.

"Dogs know their way home," I said to him. "Dogs always find their way home."

When the buffalo stopped running and they finally realized their grave mistake, the jimis would be so surprised that they would get home before us, I assured him.

Shortly afterwards we heard an angry bellow on the plains to our left. It was followed by a violent commotion. We heard angry grunts and the whining and screaming of terrified dogs.

"Hear that?" I said. The buffalo had stopped running. The jimis would soon be on their way home.

"What is he doing to them?" Nigel asked, listening to the terrible cries of the dogs.

He was scattering the jimis all over the plain with his mighty horns. That was how an enraged buffalo dealt with impudent dogs — tossing jimis in the air with their horns and stomping on them as they hit the ground. Buffalo did not bite except when they were extremely angry. And I could tell by the sound the dogs made that this buffalo was extremely angry. A buffalo could demolish a village hut with one toss of his horns.

I told Nigel everything I knew about buffalo as we

hurried across the plain. The sun was going down over the Loldaiga hills and it was getting cold. We started running.

Darkness descended as we made our way across the last stretch of forest before the Nanyuki river. Nigel was terrified. He bumped into me in his attempt to keep as close to me as possible, while I kept running into trees and things as I did not see too well in the dark.

"It's scary," Nigel finally admitted.

"Hold my hand," I told him.

When I had a good grip on his hand I said, "Now you lead and I will be with you. I can't see in the dark."

"I can't see in the dark either," he told me.

"What's wrong with your eyes?"

"Nothing," he said. "I can't see in the dark. Only animals see in the dark. Cats and dogs and such creatures."

I had to think carefully before asking, "Why are your eyes so like a cat's?"

"My mother's eyes are blue," he told me. "My father's are green. Like my grandfather's."

"But Bwana Ruin can see in the dark," I said. "Your grandfather can see in the dark."

"No, he can't. His eyes are just like mine."

A great revelation. We stumbled on.

"Can your grandfather see what I'm thinking?" I ventured.

"No."

I had to be certain.

"They say in the village that he can see into your

head," I told him. "See what people are thinking. Can he do that?"

"He cannot. No one can do that."

"But can he see in your heart?" I asked next. "Can he know when you are telling a lie?"

"No one can do that," Nigel said impatiently. "He is like other people. He can only see with his eyes."

An even greater revelation. I could not wait to get back to the village and pass on this information. The boys would never believe me.

Six

ON SUNDAYS WE went to church. Our parents never did. But we went to church on Sunday. Lesson One made sure of that with his cane.

"Lesson one!"

Thwack! went the cane on the desk.

"It does not matter that your parents are traditional," he said to us Monday mornings. "You go to church on Sunday, every Sunday, in uniform and on…?"

"Time," we yelled.

"Lesson one!"

Thwack! went the cane again.

"It does not matter that your parents are Protestants, Muslims or Catholic," he told us. "You must go to church on Sunday, in uniform and on…?"

"Time," we yelled.

Thwack!

"It does not matter if your father is a chief, a rich man or a thief," he told us. "You must go to church on Sunday in uniform and on…?"

"Time," we yelled until our ears rang.

Thwack!

So we went to church on Sundays. In the headmaster's book there was no sin greater than missing church. The church was five miles from our village, but we went to church every Sunday, in uniform and on time.

It was an old church, built by prison labor long before we were born. It was long and narrow and had a tall bell tower. The best boy in class was allowed to ring the bells for Easter Sunday. The church had stained-glass windows through which, when the light was right, one could see heaven, with the saints and the angels flying about. On the walls were pictures of saints and holy people.

The church belonged to a tidy Italian priest called Father Mario. He was in charge of all the Catholic schools and was the shortest white man I had ever seen. He was also the most fearsome, after Bwana Ruin. He once beat up a teacher for being untidy in school.

Before the service, Father Mario walked up and down the aisles where we stood — having respectfully surrendered our seats to the adults — and rapped his knuckles on every untidy head. He sent home anyone whose uniform was not fit to be in his church.

As in the village, everything in the church went according to a hierarchy. Bwana Ruin and the white people sat in the front rows. Their benches had cushions to sit on and to kneel on, while everyone else sat and kneeled on the hard wood. Our teachers sat behind the white people, with no cushions to sit on or to kneel on. The rest sat where they could — men on the right and women on the left side of the church. Girls could sit with their mothers. Boys could not sit at all. Boys had no more rights here than they had in the village.

No one ever complained. It seemed only natural that the white people, close cousins of the angels and the saints, should receive special privileges here as elsewhere in our lives.

What we boys never understood was that our headmaster, whom we all knew to be God's authority on earth, was not allowed to sit in the front row with other important people.

The Sunday I saw Nigel sitting up in front with his grandparents I was genuinely proud to be his friend. But when I tried to find out just how close he was to the saints, he had no idea what I was talking about.

Was it true, I asked, that they were all close cousins of Jesus?

"Don't be foolish," he said. "Where do you get such stupid ideas from?"

"From school."

I must have frightened him sometimes with the level of my ignorance. But my head was filled with masses of information, gathered from the village boys and from everyone else with whom I had ever had contact, that I had to verify before I could have peace.

Was it true that all mzungus were rich and had big farms and many cars? Was it true that they did not eat anything that was not sugared and sweet? Was it true that they could not lie and did not steal? Was it true that they did not bleed even if you cut them? Was it true that they were the only true people of God? Was it true that witchcraft could not kill them? Was it true that if they died they went straight to heaven?

I had so many questions, they wore Nigel out.

I learned later, from Father Mario no less, that we were all children of the same God. Not just the village boys, not just the village children, but all the children and all the people of all the world. Including Bwana Ruin and our schoolmaster, Lesson One.

But that knowledge came later.

In the meantime, Nigel fell madly in love with hunting. He wanted to go hunting every minute of every day. He came to the village three or four times a day and begged me to take him hunting. But it was the potato and bean harvesting season, and my mother kept a close rein on me.

"I'm bored," Nigel told me.

He had no one to play with.

"Go play with Salt and Pepper," I said.

But his grandfather's dogs were tired of playing fetch. He wanted to go hunting again.

"I must finish harvesting the beans," I told him.

He tried to help me finish the harvest quickly. He came by my house every chance he could and helped me with the harvest.

He was not very good at it, but he was good company as I labored and made the work seem lighter. My mother grumbled about him trampling all over her beans, but she did not know what to do with him. She did not ask him to go away. I think she liked him a little, though she did not understand a word he said. We must have harvested a whole granary together that season.

Nigel gave up his suits and started wearing khaki shorts and shirts. He took off his shoes when he was with me, and walked barefoot like me to see how it felt. I put on his shoes and walked in them to see how it felt.

In the time it took to bring in the harvest, Nigel became a regular feature around my mother's hut. The village children soon tired of following him about chanting *bwana kidogo*, little master. No one but me, it seemed, knew the white boy's name. Everyone called him simply *ka-mzungu*, little white man.

The day he ate ugali at my mother's hut was a historical event in our village. Nigel liked it and asked how it was made.

"With maize flour and water," I told him.

How did it harden? he wanted to know. It just hardened, I told him. Did she bake it in the oven? We had no oven to speak of.

"It hardens by itself," I told him.

I don't know how word got out that the little white man was eating ugali in Kariuki's mother's hut. It may have been the amazed jimis who passed it on to the village boys, who then brought along the whole village to see for themselves.

There was a sudden uproar outside. We looked up to find the whole village there, come to see Nigel eat ugali. They crowded the doorway, looked through the window and peered through the cracks in the wall. It took a long time for each and every one of them to look and wonder. To finally agree that the little white man was indeed eating ugali.

My mother was thoroughly embarrassed by their behavior. She tried in vain to drive them away.

"Have you sugared it?" they asked her.

"No," she said.

But they did not believe her.

"We want to taste it," they said.

Whereupon, her patience finally exhausted, she slammed the window in their faces. She could not shut the door. We needed the light to see by.

Nigel did not understand our language and wondered what was going on.

"Why are they staring at me?" he asked.

"You eat ugali."

"So do you."

"I am not mzungu," I told him. "They have never seen a mzungu eat ugali before."

Mzungus did not eat ugali. They lived on sweets, cakes and chocolate. I knew this to be untrue, because Father brought the evidence home from Bwana Ruin's kitchen from time to time. And Nigel had told me himself that he did not like chocolate.

But that was the story around the village.

"Do you like it?" I asked Nigel.

He loved it, he told me. It did not taste much like anything he was used to, but he loved it. He asked Mother if he could have some more. She gave us some and pleaded with the crowd to go away and leave us alone to eat our lunch. Nigel was just a hungry boy, a human being like any of them.

They refused to go away. They wanted to stand there and watch. So they remained. I began to enjoy the attention.

Eventually, word got around to my father, as he prepared lunch in Bwana Ruin's kitchen, that the white boy was eating ugali in his house. He dropped everything and came charging down to the village. He grabbed a huge chunk of firewood from the fireplace and charged at the crowd of spectators. In no time at all he had cleared the compound of all idle spectators and jimis. Then he stopped in the doorway, huffing and puffing like a rhinoceros and regarding me with eyes that burned with fury.

"Kariuki," he said. "I shall skin you today, I promise."

He was a man of few words indeed.

"Come," he said, taking Nigel by the hand. "Your food is ready."

Nigel was too startled to argue as father dragged him out of the hut and through the village to his grandfather's house where, no doubt, nice things waited to be eaten.

My day of fame and glory turned to mud. Why did

everything that was fun turn out to be like a deliberate effort to have my father dismissed from his job?

Nigel did not come back that day.

When my chores were done, I called Jimi and we went for a walk along the river. We ended up by my duck pool and sat for hours listening to the water rush over the rocks. Jimi eventually got bored and went back home, leaving me to brood alone.

I could smell buffalo stealing through the forest. But I saw nothing and heard nothing.

The duck family did not come out to play that day and I was worried about them. Had they been killed and eaten by some wild animals? Or had they moved to another part of the river where it was safer?

I waited for them until sunset.

That night at about midnight, Father came back from Bwana Ruin's kitchen and woke me up roughly. He found me in the middle of a nightmare and, when I opened my eyes and saw him looming over me, I thought he had finally made up his mind to take me out in the forest and skin me alive.

"Mother," I cried in panic.

"Quiet," he said.

"Hari," I called out.

"Shut up," Father ordered.

"Mother," I cried. "He is killing me!"

He gave me a hard slap that nearly knocked my head off my shoulders. It shocked me into silence long enough to hear what he had to say.

"Get up," he ordered.

The fire was burning bright, throwing grotesque shadows on the wall. We were alone in the room, just the two of us. Hari slept in his own hut next to the grain store. Mother and Father slept in the next room.

We were in the kitchen. That was where I slept, on a platform of sticks and boards. It was a hard and rough bed. But I was always so tired when I went to bed that I did not feel a thing.

"Get dressed," Father said.

There was no doubt left in my mind any more. He intended to finally carry out his threat of skinning me alive. But why was Mother so quiet? Didn't she care about me at all? I knew she loved me. Why didn't she come to my rescue?

Then it hit me. He had killed her too and left her in the forest for the hyenas.

I was trembling all over when I got out of bed. I stood before him and awaited my fate.

"Sit down," he said.

I sat down on a stool across the fire from him. He had taken off his white uniform and changed into his brown shirt and patched cord trousers. Except for the tortured look in his eye, he seemed just like my father.

He took a piece of cake he had brought back from the kitchen and gave it to me.

"Eat," he ordered.

He found a foul-smelling piece of cigarette and lit it. From the riverside came the terrible scream of the tree hyrax. The sound had frightened Nigel half to death the first time he heard it as we came back from hunting. Then he had told me that the hyrax was a true cousin of the elephant. He had read it in a book.

"I want to talk to you," my father said.

I ate my cake and listened. He was as bad with emotions as he was with words. I could never tell what he felt for me. I could not tell if he felt anything at all. All I knew was that I could never please him, no matter how hard I tried.

Finally he sorted out his words.

"Keep away from the little white man," he said.

"Why?"

"Why?" His right hand rose, ready to bounce me off the wall of the hut. Then he remembered he wanted to talk, not fight.

"Do you want to have me dismissed from my job?" he asked.

"No." It was the last thing in the world I wanted.

"Then keep away from the boy."

And that was that. Our little talk seemed over. He pulled on his cigarette. I polished off the last of my cake and got ready to go back to bed. Then he stirred suddenly and cleared his throat.

"Kariuki," he said with great difficulty. "White people are not like us. They do not want us to step on their clean floors. I must take off my shoes when I step in their kitchen to do my work. They do not want us to touch their things. They say we make them dirty. They do not like us. They do not want our children to play with their children. They are not like us at all. They do not want their children to eat our food."

"Why?" I asked.

"Why?" he repeated. "Because… they hate us."

"Why?"

"Why?" He had to think a long while. Even then, the answer he gave was no more illuminating than anything else he ever told me.

"They could die," he said finally.

"Why?" I asked.

"Why?" he repeated. "Because… they are not like us."

He pulled on his cigarette. I had never had this much conversation with him before. I was thrilled. His long, thoughtful pauses were very impressive, very profound.

Somewhere in my heart, deep down under the layers and layers of fear and awe and absolute terror, I had a certain pride in and respect for my father.

"They are not used to our food," he said finally.

"Nigel eats ugali," I said reasonably.

"He must not eat ugali."

"Why?" I asked.

"Why?" His hand rose instinctively.

Any discussion we had ever had before had involved some sort of violent physical contact. His knuckles on my bare head.

He now lowered his hand and said, "Because…"

He had great difficulty getting at whatever he wanted to tell me. His eyes, his will, his whole being pleaded with me to help by understanding at once.

"Do you know what they do with ugali?" he asked me.

I had no idea.

"They give it to their dogs," he told me.

So what? We gave ugali to our dogs too.

He nodded in agreement and said that was not the point. That was completely different. It was not the same as giving it to the little white boy at all.

"Do you know what would happen to me if he should fall ill and die?" he said fearfully.

I had no idea.

"I would be fired," he said. "I would lose my job."

And that was not all. They would take him out and hang him. Then they would come for my mother and take her out and hang her too.

"And then," as if that was not enough to scare me already, "then they would come for you. And Hari."

My father did not make up the stories to frighten me. He believed every word. I had to believe too. The fear in his eyes was all too real.

He made me promise never to give ugali to the white boy again.

I promised. But he wanted more than that. He wanted me to also promise not to play with or to have anything at all to do with the little white man.

I promised. I did not believe he expected me to keep such a promise.

"Go to bed," he ordered.

I gladly climbed back on my platform. I was thoroughly exhausted by our discussion and fell asleep right away.

There was one very bad outcome of the whole ugali affair. The village boys now knew that the little white man was human too. From that day on, every village bully wanted to test his strength and enhance his reputation by wrestling Nigel to the ground and thrashing the daylights out of him. I had a hard time protecting him, and on occasion got thoroughly beaten myself.

Seven

THEY COULD NOT keep Nigel away from my compound. I was his only friend, but I never gave him ugali again.

He came by every chance he got and pleaded with me to take him hunting. He could not understand how I wasn't even supposed to be with him.

We sat in the yard and played marbles as I thought of a dozen things to keep our minds occupied and away from his first and only love, hunting. Whenever he brought up the subject I had to invent good excuses like the jimis were sick or Jimi had gone off to Nanyuki with Hari. Sometimes his grandfather took him on a different kind of hunt. They went far out into the plains in the roofless Land Rover to where the game was plentiful. There was no running, not even walking. They drove up, stopped the vehicle and, while the animals watched and wondered, Bwana Ruin stood on the seat and shot them dead. Then he loaded them on the vehicle and brought them back for his dogs.

"You don't eat the meat?" I asked Nigel.

MEJA MWANGI

"Grandma can't stand the smell of game," he told me.

My mother couldn't stand the smell of fish.

"Crocodile?" he asked.

I told him we didn't bother with any animals we could not eat.

"Zebra?"

I had never heard of anyone who ate zebras. But Nigel had read about it in a book. Some people even ate snakes.

"Tastes like rabbit," he said.

"I have eaten rabbit."

"Buffalo?"

"Tastes like beef," I said.

"I have never eaten buffalo," he said.

Bwana Ruin killed buffalo all the time, I informed him. We ate buffalo often.

"Have you ever eaten warthog?" I asked.

"How does it taste?"

All I could remember was the smell.

We were sitting by the chicken run next to Hari's hut, on buckets with holes in them and brown with rust. I wanted to go swimming, but Nigel wanted to hunt.

"Bwana Ruin does not want you to go with me," I told him. "My father told me that."

"Nonsense," he said. "He didn't say not to go hunting. He told me not to come to the village."

"Bwana Ruin will be angry," I said.

"I have no one at the house," he told me. "Only my grandma, and she doesn't let me touch anything. She thinks I'll hurt myself. It's so boring."

"Does she beat you?"

"Never."

"My father beats me sometimes," I informed him. "I have to be very careful what I do or say around him."

"Dad would never touch me," he told me.

"What about your mother?"

"Never, ever."

My mother never touched me either. But her bark was much worse than her bite.

"Grandma's like that," Nigel said.

"Do you like her?"

He thought hard about it, shrugged and said, "I don't know. She's nice and all but…"

"What about your father?" I asked.

"He's the greatest."

It was quite a revelation. I never expected to find a boy, even a mzungu one, who liked his father. I had been led to believe boys weren't supposed to understand, let alone like their fathers. Just to fear them and keep out of their way.

"I like my brother Hari," I told him. He beat me too, sometimes, but he was still my best friend. "He taught me to fish and hunt."

Nigel remembered about hunting.

"Couldn't we go just once more? I'll be going back to school soon," he told me.

"I don't know," I said. I didn't want my father to lose his job. He'd kill me for that.

Nigel didn't want me to be killed either so we forgot about hunting. We could smell the ugali my mother was preparing for lunch.

Could he have some ugali?

I had no wish to see my parents hang.

"Let's go hunting," I said.

I called Jimi from under the grain store. He didn't want to come with us. He was still angry with me for letting him get into an argument with a wild buffalo. I apologized for this, although even a blind dog would have known the difference between hare and buffalo, and assured him it would not happen again. Today we would go after Old Moses.

He summoned his friends and any other village dog that would come, and we set off for the adventure of our lives. With fifteen dogs in tow, we sneaked behind the village to avoid meeting my father or Nigel's grandfather.

Children came to call out "little white man." Nigel ignored them. The bigger boys objected to our taking their dogs hunting and wanted to fight us, but we had no time for fights. We had a long way to go. Other jimis saw us and tagged along. By the time we crossed the first river we had a mob of thirty dogs or more.

We swept through the forest like a storm, searched under every log and bush, sniffed in every nook and cranny, and made enough noise to scare all the animals away. We didn't find any animals in the forest. They could hear us coming from miles away.

Scents criss-crossed like a finely woven net in the undergrowth. The jimis got very confused and excited. But we stayed together like a wind-driven storm until we came out on the open grassy plateau between the rivers.

Here was our first big challenge.

Hares popped up everywhere. Scared like rabbits they raced round and round, popping in and out of holes like magic. In spite of our pleas the dogs went after them with enthusiasm. Soon we had dogs burrowing into rabbit holes all over the plain, and turning up all sorts of surprises. They found two poisonous snakes, a fox, a wild cat and a tired old hyena who didn't have the guts to fight and took off for the forest as fast as he could run.

There was only one possible solution to this anarchy. I grabbed Hari's dog and slipped my belt around his neck. Then I led him forcefully across the plain and down to the Liki forest. Most of the other dogs came with us. They would follow Hari's jimi anywhere. I had no doubt the rest would eventually follow us too as soon as they realized the futility of digging into the maze of rabbit holes that ran under the plain. A rabbit could go for miles under the ground without surfacing even once. I had learned this since our last hunt from my brother Hari, an old hand at hunting.

We swept through the Liki forest to emerge, hours

later, on the Loldaiga plain, a seemingly endless grass plateau. It was flat and even all the way to the Loldaiga hills. The grass was taller and more profuse. Wild game flourished and thrived here, away from the farmlands and the farmers' cattle.

Zebras, gazelles and giraffes moved freely in numerous herds spreading in their thousands far to the horizon. There were lions and wild dogs too, but we didn't see any of them.

We had a hard time convincing the dogs they couldn't possibly catch any of them. The plains game had the whole world to run away to. I gave Jimi to Nigel to hang on to, for he too was of the opinion we should go after the gazelles. Then I climbed a gnarled old acacia tree so I could see over the grass.

I searched all around for Old Moses, but he was nowhere to be seen. The plain around his territory seemed bare. I was afraid he may have died or moved to another part of the world. I already knew that warthogs were territorial. Once they found an area they liked and established a house, they lived near the burrow until they died. They never strayed farther than they could run straight back into their hole.

Then I saw him, lying in the grass in a mound like an anthill. He was about a quarter of a mile away, not far from where I knew his hole was. I climbed down.

"Have you seen him?" Nigel asked eagerly.

"He is sleeping."

"Why? It's still light."

"Maybe he is tired. Animals sleep whenever they feel like."

Jimi pricked his ears to catch our words. I took the belt from Nigel and led Jimi in the direction of the sleeping warthog. If we surprised him in his sleep, then maybe we had a chance.

I led the way, tiptoeing through the grass, stopping now and then to listen. All I could hear were the dogs roving through the bush and making enough noise to wake the entire plain.

We pressed on a little faster now to get to our quarry before the other jimis did. Many of them had strayed so far off course there was little chance they would find us again today.

"Why is he called Old Moses?" Nigel wanted to know.

"He is the oldest warthog in the world," I said. He was also the meanest. "You will see."

I should have known there would be no surprising Old Moses that day. Not with so many dogs blundering through the plain. When we came to where I had seen him sleeping, Old Moses was up on his short, sturdy legs, facing our way and waiting to see who came out of the tall grass.

"Wow!" Nigel was totally amazed. "What is that?"

"Old Moses."

He was big, almost as big as a buffalo, and he had thick black-brown skin that was bald with age. He had short powerful legs, a massive head with warts as big as pumpkins and a long tapered face with tufts of black hair on the crown. His mean little eyes were almost closed in concentration.

But the most impressive feature of the old warthog were his teeth. His huge, strangely curved saber tusks were amber brown, and they swept out of the sides of his mouth and curved forwards, outwards and upwards for almost a foot on either side of his head.

"Wow!" Nigel said. "He is big!"

"Watch out," I told him. "He is also dangerous."

We stood there and eyed each other. I could feel Jimi trembling by my side. It wasn't from fear. I had taught Jimi to be fearless, but he too was impressed by the size of the creature in front of us.

I released him, taking the leash from his neck. He remained by my side, one leg raised, undecided whether to commit himself. He studied the situation. Meanwhile, the other jimis had no idea where we were.

Old Moses snorted and shook his massive head at us in warning. We stood our ground. After a moment of this threatening behavior, he approached, slowly, with measured steps.

"Jimi?" I said quietly. "Go get him, boy!"

Jimi was still thinking about it. He was no ordinary dog.

Old Moses quickened his pace.

"Jimi?"

"He's scared," said Nigel.

"Jimi is not scared of anything," I informed him.

Old Moses was moving faster now, his bouncing

motion building momentum. Soon he would be in full charge. Then only a tree could stop him.

"Jimi!" Nigel's voice rose in panic.

Jimi stood his ground.

Any second now, Old Moses would knock us across the plain, unless Jimi did something about it, fast.

Jimi started his own charge too late. We could see that, but not him. They met twenty feet from us, the warthog going full steam. There was a mighty crash, and our Jimi went flying into the air and disappeared in the grass behind us.

I grabbed Nigel's hand, ready to run for it. Then the warthog braked suddenly, stopping in a cloud of dust ten feet from us. He whirled around, searching for his adversary. We could hear Jimi groaning behind the bushes.

"Wow!" said Nigel. "Did you see that!"

I had seen it all right, and I knew what it meant. Our defence was gone. We had just been defeated, while the rest of our army of dogs wandered the plains in search of adventure. The hunt was over before it had begun.

There was only one course of action left now. Leave Old Moses alone, collect Hari's Jimi — whatever was left of him — and go home to plan another day.

I was considering this line of action when two of Jimi's best friends happened along and, without waiting to find out what was going on, went straight for Old Moses.

The old warthog was just as startled as we were. He too had considered the skirmish over and won. But he was a mean old fighter. He went back into battle with determination.

More jimis turned up, drawn by the noise, and they joined in. Old Moses was outnumbered, but none of the dogs could match his speed or strength. He snorted, grunted and whirled at top speed, tossing the tenacious little mongrels this way and that. Then he turned around and, with his little tail pointed at the sky, crashed through the bushes in full flight.

The dogs went after him. Jimi emerged from the bushes, still a little dizzy from the fall, and charged after the mob. We came last, running as fast as we could to keep up.

We went through the tall grass to a patch of open ground where the dogs started gaining on the warthog. By then a band of at least twenty strong jimis had converged on the quarry, going like the wind and raising such a din that we must have been heard all the way across the plain.

Old Moses charged on, his short legs pumping, the massive head swinging from side to side to keep the pursuers in sight. Whenever the dogs got too close for comfort he would whirl around without breaking stride and scatter them on the dust. Then he would take off again, fast as lightning. But we could see he was getting tired. His pace was slackening and his snorts and grunts came less forcefully.

We pressed on, yelling at the dogs to get him. With Jimi now back in the lead, it seemed a certainty.

Then, all of a sudden, as the dogs were gathering their last energies for the kill, Old Moses stopped and turned around to face us. The jimis were so surprised by this that instead of pouncing on him immediately and bringing him to his knees, they paused too, wondering what was on his mind.

Then Old Moses moved. Not forwards, as the dogs expected, but backwards, moving at such an incredible speed that he left us breathless. By the time the dogs figured out what was happening, the warthog was safely in his hole laughing his head off.

Then the jimis charged forward and crashed at the mouth of the hole, fighting to be the first to go in after him. They piled up at the entrance and would have suffocated had I not taken a stick and beaten sense into the pack. They stood back and waited. I asked for volunteers. They all volunteered. All except Jimi. He was older and wiser.

We picked the leanest volunteer, an eager little jimi with no brains at all. We pushed him head first into the old warthog's castle. He went in easily, wriggling his way in with amazing enthusiasm. Then we stood back and waited to see what would happen.

He was gone for a few seconds. Then we heard a muffled rumbling underground followed by a terrified yelp. Then the dog shot backwards out of the hole. He went spinning into the air and landed in a cloud of dust several yards away. He lay there as if dead.

There were no more volunteers after that.

We had quite quickly reached what could be called a stalemate. The warthog stayed inside and we stayed outside.

I asked for smart ideas. Jimi thought we should go back home. The other jimis thought we should go after the gazelles and the plains animals they could see grazing miles away on the horizon.

"No use," I told them. They were looking at the survivors of many more serious hunts by predators that were much smarter and more determined than any jimi. Lions, wild dogs and hyenas had all, at one time or another, gone after the gazelles. But the jimis were welcome to try.

"But don't say I did not warn you."

They grumbled, but they stayed with us.

"Let's smoke him out," Nigel suggested.

It sounded like a good idea, and it was our only idea, so we gathered twigs and dry grass, piled them over the hole and lit them. But the wind was blowing the wrong way, and it blew the smoke in our faces instead. After a few attempts we gave it up.

Soon the dogs got bored and wandered into the bushes to look for something more interesting.

"Any bright ideas?" I asked Nigel.

"We wait for him to get hungry."

"Could take days."

We didn't have days. We didn't even have hours. Night was coming. Now that I knew Nigel did not see in the dark, I worried about darkness.

"We'll get Salt and Pepper," he said. "They are not afraid of anything."

"It will be dark before we get home," I told him.

We wondered what to do.

A pack of jimis got it into their heads to go after the gazelles. I tried to hold them back, told them it would be dark before they got to where the gazelles were, and by then the gazelles would be somewhere else equally far away. But they chose not to believe me and went on their way.

We rounded up the remaining dogs and headed home. Along the way we ate some wild berries, but they did little to relieve our hunger.

The sun went down as we made our way through the forest. I could smell buffalo but, not wanting to frighten Nigel, I did not mention it. Nor did I tell him of the shadows that lurked, watching us go by, following us with their eyes. The dogs saw them too but they knew them for what they were and did not bark.

A subdued cough betrayed their presence to Nigel. He clutched my arm, his hand cold with fear.

"What's that?"

"Nothing," I said loudly for the shadows to hear. I was a good boy who saw nothing and said nothing.

The fear grew, mounting with every step we took until it was too great to bear.

Then we ran, and we did not stop until we got home.

The following day I told Hari I had seen his friends in the forest.

"My friends?" he asked.

"The ones who gave me the letter to bring to you. The men of the forest."

Hari glanced around, saw that no one was watching and pulled me behind the chicken house.

"What did they say to you?" he asked.

"Nothing."

"Did they give you another letter?"

"No."

"Did they talk to you at all?

"No."

"Then why are you telling me about them?"

I had thought he might want to know, I told him. I wanted to be his friend.

He pinched me by the ears and lifted me off my feet. I bit my lip, determined not to cry out from the pain. When he finally put me down, he gave me a left-right slap and I went deaf.

From that day on I never told Hari anything he didn't ask to know.

Eight

BOYS ARE OFTEN the first to know when things go wrong. When lions invaded Bwana Ruin's cattle bomas and ate three of his biggest bulls, it was a boy who first came across the feasting lions and raised the alarm. When fire suddenly gutted the old storage barns where Bwana Ruin stored his diesel and hay, it was a boy who was the first to see the smoke. And when the old watchman disappeared from the dairy, where the machines were also stolen, it was a boy who came upon his body buried in the forest, far away from the farmstead, and alerted everyone about it.

I knew that the white farmers lived a good and rich life in the big farmhouses, while the Africans who labored for them lived a life of slavery in their crumbling village huts. I knew white people did not like black people and treated them little better than donkeys and much worse than their dogs. My father had told me as much. I knew they paid their workers a pittance and worked them like slaves. I knew that white people beat black people and locked them up in police cells. I knew that they sent black people on detention to faraway islands where they died of malaria and other diseases. It was no secret that Bwana Ruin beat up and abused the village women when he found them in the forest cutting trees for firewood.

I knew these things and more, because people talked about them all the time. Once Bwana Ruin had set his dogs loose on us when he found us stealing fruit from his orchard. I had escaped by jumping over an impossibly tall keiapple fence, but one boy died from the mauling he got from the dogs. His father had to run two miles to the hospital carrying his gravely injured son on his back, because Bwana Ruin had refused to allow Hari to take the boy to hospital on the ox cart that transported milk and cream to Nanyuki.

"A thief is a thief," he had said. "Let it be a lesson."

But we soon forgot and went back to raiding his orchard. It was the only fruit garden around.

Though I knew these things, and many more things that were wrong and unjust, I never let them worry me for a moment. They had been going on for a long time, and the adults had done nothing but grumble about them. Besides, I had school to go to and fish to catch and Old Moses to hunt. So I left it to the grownups to moan about the injustices.

Even my own father was helpless. He grumbled, he moaned and, in extreme cases, he took out his anger on me or Hari. When things went very wrong in the kitchen, when he burned the roast and got a lashing from Mamsab Ruin, he came home raging. He looked for something we had done, or not done, and gave us a beating for it. He lay awake at night, tossing angrily in his bed and sighing again and again. I heard him swear not to take it any more. I heard him promise himself to stand up for his rights and his dignity. I heard him swear to resign and find another job.

From my hard and cold bed in the cooking place, I heard my father do a lot of thinking out loud. But, come morning, he rose with the roosters and went to light the woodstove in the kitchen and heat the bath water for Bwana Ruin. No matter what sort of a night my father had, Bwana Ruin's breakfast was always ready by seven o'clock.

I knew there were gangs of men living in the forest and armed with machetes and spears and smelling like old buffalos. I knew them to be the mau-mau. According to Bwana Ruin, they were bad men, thieves and murderers. They had never stolen anything from me or spoken to me, apart from the day they gave me a message for Hari.

I knew I must not talk about them to anyone, not even to Hari who was their friend. But I did not have the vaguest idea what they were about, or why they crept through the shadows in the forest. It was not until the second raid by the white soldiers that I began to get an idea of what was going on.

The soldiers rounded us all up and herded us into the old auction pen as before. They made us sit on the cow dung. They surrounded us, their guns pointed at our heads while they ransacked our village again. They searched every nook and cranny, looking for anything that would link the villagers to the mau-mau. They turned the huts inside out and stole money and valuables as they had done before. But they found no guns and no sign of mau-mau, and they gave up the search in the end.

Bwana Ruin came to address his people and plead with them to be cooperative. He stood on the auctioneer's platform way above our heads so that the sun burned our eyes when we looked up at him. He surveyed us like a herd of cattle and addressed our upturned faces.

"*Watu*," he said, "I hear there are some *watu* going about at night telling you a lot of *maneno*, a lot of nonsense."

He was dressed in his khakis and riding boots. As usual he rapped on his right boot with his riding crop as he spoke.

He was not angry this time. The soldiers had allowed his cook and other essential personnel to go to work as usual before leading the rest into the auction pen. He had not kept us waiting as long as he had the last time. But the mothers had learned from the earlier experience, when children had cried themselves sick, so they had brought enough to eat and to drink. It felt more like a forced picnic than a military operation.

Bwana Ruin arrived after his usual inspection of the farm.

"This is my land," he said forcefully. "Bought from the Crown and paid for with my own money. If the mau-mau tell you that they will take it from me and give it to you or to anyone else, they are telling you a load of manure. That will never happen. Not in two thousand years. Not over my dead body."

Mamsab Ruin and the little white man watched the proceedings from a distance. Nigel caught my eye and waved. I dared not wave back.

"Freedom?" Bwana Ruin was saying. "What freedom, *aye*? I ask you again, what freedom are they telling you about? Freedom to do what? Freedom to go where? You *watu* know you have nowhere else to go. Your tribal reserves are overflowing with poor and unemployed people. You have no land to go back to. *Kweli rongo?* True or not?"

"*Kweli*," the workers answered. "Too true."

"You know that I have been very good to you," he went on. "I have given you a job and a generous salary. More than other bwanas pay their labor. You ask their watu. They will tell you I am the best bwana in Nanyuki. I have given you a place to live. Very soon I shall demol-ish your old hovels and build you new ones. I give you a pound of *posho* and all the skimmed milk you can drink. *Kweli rongo?*"

"*Kweli*," some people said. Others nodded in agree-ment.

The sun was very hot now and we prayed he would soon let us go back to our business. Then the jimis showed up. The village dogs, we were to discover, had taken the opportunity to ransack the wide-open huts after the soldiers had left. They had eaten all the food they could find, all the milk and several sitting hens and numerous eggs. Now Jimi came by to see what had happened to the owners of the vandalized huts. He was accompanied by two of his loyal lieutenants, two lazy old jimis who hung around with him because he seemed to know where to eat.

On seeing the armed soldiers guarding us, the dogs ran into the bush and returned to the village.

I could see Nigel was impatient. He walked nervously around his grandmother. He squatted. He got up and walked around her again.

We had set this day aside for the adventure of our lives. Today we were to forget the worthless village dogs and take Salt and Pepper hunting instead. They were our last card against Old Moses, the indomitable old man of the plain. But this mau-mau business was taking too long.

"Freedom, *aye*?" Bwana Ruin raved. "You *watu* know you are free to come and go as you wish. You are not my prisoners here. You are not my slaves here, *aye*? You can leave any time you wish. You may leave today, if you wish. Who wants to leave, right now? Hands up those who want to leave."

A few hands went up, but they were all from bored children who had no idea what he was talking about. They wanted to go back home to play.

Their mothers whacked their hands down.

"So you all want to stay and work for me, *aye*?" Bwana Ruin asked.

"*Ndiyo*, Bwana," the people said as one. "Yes, Bwana."

"Very well," he told them. "But remember that no matter what they tell you, this land will never be yours. Not in two thousand years."

He said he intended to farm the land until he died. Then his children would farm it and his grandchildren too. But, as long as they worked well, the watu and their wives and totos would be free to live and work for him. They would be treated well and they would always get their wages. That was a guarantee from Bwana Ruin.

"You go tell them that," he said in conclusion. "You go tell your mau-mau brothers what I have told you today. They don't know what they are playing with."

He turned abruptly and hopped down from the platform. He talked with the officers for a moment. Then he left for his house.

Without a word to the villagers, the soldiers climbed back on their trucks and drove away. They did not arrest anyone this time and it took the villagers a while to realize that they had been dismissed and could go back home. Then there was a general scramble back to the village to see what had survived the invasion of the white soldiers.

It took the villagers the rest of the afternoon to sort out the mess. The dogs had turned the place upside down. In some instances they had carried household articles from one end of the village to the other and left them there.

The villagers had learned from the last time around, and they had hidden their money well. In their desperation to find the money they knew was hidden somewhere, the soldiers had stopped just short of dismantling the huts.

Some villagers had done such a thorough job of hiding their money that they never found it again. For months after this second invasion, money kept turning up in the strangest places long after the owners had forgotten about it.

I left my mother searching desperately for the money she had hidden in the thatched roof of the latrine and sneaked through the village. I avoided Jimi so he would not know what I was up to and made a wide detour to our agreed meeting point by the fish pond.

Nigel was there with Salt and Pepper, holding the dogs by their collars so they would not get bored and go back home. They were massive German shepherds and came up to his waist.

"What was that all about?" he asked me.

"Nothing," I told him. "The soldiers do that from time to time."

"What was my grandfather talking to you about?" he asked.

"I don't know," I said. "Did you bring the biscuits?"

His pockets were stuffed with them. We were both

beginning to understand that we could not catch, skin, roast and eat Old Moses all in one busy day.

The dogs growled at me. They were wondering what I was doing there.

"Shut up," Nigel ordered.

I was his friend, he told them. They were to leave me alone, otherwise he would give them a hiding like they had never received before.

I was very impressed by his authority. I had nothing but fearful respect for those giant dogs, and I was a whole year older than Nigel.

"We must hurry," I told him.

He dragged the dogs by their leashes and we forded the river. We cut as straight a path as possible through the forest. The ground rose unevenly through the rock-strewn undergrowth, and the dogs wanted to go their separate ways. Nigel could hardly cope as they pulled in different directions. He tried to give one of them to me to hold on to. But the dog wanted to eat me up on the spot and I was scared stiff of him. So Nigel had to hang on to both dogs until we got to the grassland plateau between the two rivers, and the dogs forgot all about going back home.

The going was easier on the grassland. The dogs ranged out ahead of us, making us feel safer than we had felt on any hunt before. They got excited when they ran across ten different animal scents and could not decide which one to follow. Nigel managed to get them back on course and we made good time over the plateau. We crossed the Liki valley to the Loldaiga plain.

It was late afternoon by then. Rain clouds were gathering over the mountains to the east. But we did not have to worry about those. We would be safely back home before the first drops fell.

Or so I thought.

We did not have time to waste worrying about the weather. We got straight down to business — finding Old Moses. Now that we knew where to look, it did not take us long.

He was grazing peacefully in the shade of a spreading acacia tree, staying out of the hot afternoon sun. He saw us coming from way off and stopped grazing to watch us. He was old and short-sighted and did not make us out until we were about two hundred yards from him. We were busy trying to point him out to the dogs and not doing too well. The plain was crowded with game. Zebras, giraffes, gazelles and wildebeests browsed quietly and ignored us completely.

When we came to about a hundred yards from him, Old Moses snorted, raised his tail in alarm and did a wild dust-raising dance where he stood. He made a complete circle around the tree and pawed the ground in warning. We stopped to watch. He feigned a charge at us, covering about thirty yards in a short fast trot, before stopping to paw the ground again. He shook his giant head at us and rattled his saber teeth, daring us to come closer.

This was a mistake, because Salt and Pepper finally

noticed him. They stopped dead in their tracks. Their ears pricked dangerously, and they watched the antics of this strange creature that was neither pig nor dog and that had teeth growing outside its mouth. They had never gone hunting before. They were guard dogs. They had no idea what a warthog was.

They took a few steps forward, stopped and watched Old Moses dance with excitement. Then they leaped forward and charged across the grassland. Old Moses charged too, coming at them at top speed and shaking the ground with his weight. We held our breath and stood back to watch.

About ten yards from the animal, the dogs started to slow down. The full ugliness of the creature finally dawned on them. Close up, the warthog was even more fearsome.

The dogs were beginning to have second thoughts about attacking Old Moses when, unable to stop his own charge, he crashed into them full force and sent them flying.

Then he charged toward us at full speed.

I cried out in terror and scrambled out of his way. Nigel had started running the moment the dogs went flying into the air. He was racing like mad the way we had come and screaming his head off.

Old Moses went for him. I ran after Old Moses, trying to think what I should do if I caught up with him. Salt and Pepper recovered from their shock and raced after us.

They overtook me, going like the wind and baying for the creature's blood.

I slowed down to watch. Old Moses was so intent on demolishing Nigel that he had no idea we were after him. He was snorting at his heels, ready to fling him into the air with one toss of his giant tusks, when the dogs caught up with him. They hit him from behind with the combined force of their full charge.

I watched in amazement as the giant creature stumbled and went cartwheeling in the air to land with a thunderous crash a foot from Nigel's legs. The dogs, just as stunned, landed on top of him.

He rolled back onto his legs and took off in the opposite direction. He came full tilt at me, shaking his head from side to side and trying to dislodge the clumps of earth and grass stuck to his tusks. I cried out and jumped out of his way. The dogs chased after him, charging at an uncontrollable speed. I chased after the dogs.

We pursued Old Moses for about three hundred yards before he finally slowed down and stopped. He turned round to face us and waved his tusks at us. Salt and Pepper stopped too. They were aware by now that this was no ordinary creature they were up against.

I walked up to them and stopped. Then, without warning, Old Moses moved. We had all expected him to charge forward. He moved backwards instead, reversing into his burrow at such a speed that the ground shook when he crashed into the bottom of the hole.

Nigel ran up breathless and shaking with terror. He was covered in dust from head to boot.

"Where did he go?" he asked.

"Home," I said.

Salt and Pepper were just as confounded by the warthog's disappearing trick. Then they discovered the hole in the ground and, in their excitement, tried to get into it together. They got stuck in the entrance. We pulled them out and Salt started digging straight away, his paws scattering earth in all directions. We stood back to watch him dig.

"Will he come out again?" Nigel asked.

I didn't think so. Not today, anyway.

"Wow!" Nigel was ecstatic. "Did you see that?"

"Are you still scared?"

"Not any more."

"But you are shaking."

"I'm all right," he said. "I'm quite all right."

Then his legs could no longer support him, and he had to sit down. His face was streaked with sweat and dust. He put on a brave face but I could see that he was very frightened.

"Did you bring the knife?" he wanted to know.

I had forgotten about the knife. The business with the soldiers had upset too many plans.

"How shall we skin him?" he asked.

I did not wish to disappoint him, but I thought I had better set him straight.

"We are not going to catch Old Moses."

"We have him in the hole," he argued. "Where can he go?"

"We have to get him out of there first, see? It's not so easy."

"The dogs will dig him out."

I liked Nigel. He was fun to be with and he had lots of good ideas. But his ignorance was wearisome sometimes.

I explained to him how deep a warthog's hole was. It would take Salt and Pepper a month or two to dig down to Old Moses.

Nigel did not believe me, but he did not argue.

"We'll smoke the monster out," he said, taking out his matches.

But the wind was blowing in the wrong direction. The sun was ready to set over the hills, but the dogs went on digging, taking it in turns to widen the entrance to the hole. Every now and then Old Moses gave a warning grunt from deep inside the hole, a deep rumbling sound as of distant thunder.

"I think we should go home now," I said to Nigel. "We can come back early tomorrow."

"Just a few more minutes," he said. "We are nearly there now."

We were not, but I didn't argue with him. I sat down. We talked about this and that and waited for the dogs to give up. We ate some biscuits, scooping them out of Nigel's pockets in handfuls. The running and the falling about had broken them to powder.

We sat there a long time while the dogs dug.

Unnoticed by us, thunder rolled from the mountain and down the river valleys.

Nine

WHEN THE ENTRANCE to the warthog's hole was wide enough, Salt pushed his head and shoulders through and barked in the hole.

There was a sudden quiet from within. We got down on our knees and put our ears to the ground to listen. We heard the sound we had heard once before, the rumbling of approaching thunder. The sound grew louder as it came nearer, and the earth shook.

We jumped to our feet and prepared to run. Then Salt gave a yelp. He shot backwards out of the hole and went spinning in the air. He crashed into Pepper and both dogs went down in a cloud of dust.

Old Moses stuck his head out of the burrow and shook his tusks at us. Then he retreated and crashed to the bottom of the hole with a thud.

The dogs picked themselves up from the dust. They were shivering from the shock. Salt limped over to Nigel, but Pepper dove angrily into the hole, pushing his way in until only his tail was left wagging in the air.

Again the deep, expectant silence. Pepper was older

and wiser than Salt. He did not bark in the hole. He listened, as we did, to the start of the rumbling that would warn us of the approaching thunder.

We heard it coming, the ground shaking from its force, and we jumped back as before.

Pepper wriggled out of the hole and sprang away from the mouth of the den at the very last second.

With a loud whooshing sound, Old Moses shot out of the hole and into the air. Pepper had timed the moment just right. He leapt onto the old warthog's back and sank his teeth into the massive mane. They landed ten yards away from us. Pepper was still on top, trying desperately to sink his killer fangs into the warthog's thick neck.

Old Moses charged on through the grassland. We waited for him to turn around and come charging back to his den.

It took us a moment to realize that he had no intention of returning to his hole. Then we ran.

Salt had by now fully recovered from shock and he dashed forward to help his brother.

Then Old Moses stopped so suddenly that Pepper flew off his back and went crashing into the dust. Old Moses veered to the right and made for the first line of bush, about half a mile away along the river valley. When the dust cleared, we saw Pepper pick himself up and go furiously after Old Moses, with Salt right behind him.

We ran after them. I stepped into a mole hole and fell down. Nigel was fifty paces behind me and doing his

best to keep up. I stopped to wait for him. He was panting heavily, and his arms and his legs were almost black
with sweat and dust.

"Shall we go home now?" I asked while he caught his
breath.

"No." His face was red with excitement. "We almost
have him now."

"But he is gone. We'll never see him again."

"We shall," he said. "The dogs will catch him now."

"It will be dark soon," I pleaded. "We must go home."

He looked around and for the first time seemed to
realize where he was. The sun was sinking over the hills
and we were still miles away from home. Way up in the
east, thunderclouds poured from the mountains into
the valleys. Lightning flashed and thunder clashed.
There was the smell of dust in the air, a sign that the rain
had started its gradual descent into the plains.

I worried about flash floods. I worried about the
river flooding.

"We must go home now," I said to Nigel.

"But the dogs," he said. "We must get the dogs."

"It will soon be dark," I told him.

"We must get the dogs," he insisted. "We can't go
home without them."

We ran on.

The old warthog had disappeared in the forest. Salt
and Pepper dove in after him. We came up to the first
line of trees.

I stepped on a thorn and sat down to take it out. It

was a long and hard acacia thorn and it had gone right through my foot. I called to Nigel to stop and help me take it out, but he had already disappeared into the forest after the dogs.

I gritted my teeth and yanked out the thorn. Then I rubbed leaves on the wound to stop the bleeding. My foot was extremely painful. I could not run any more.

I called out for Nigel. There was no reply. I limped into the forest after him. It was gloomy and silent except for the crickets now rising to sing their eerie night songs.

The sudden silence was frightening. With growing panic, I finally woke up to something that had been nagging me since the whole affair with Old Moses had started. It was the silent and savage way the Alsatian dogs had gone after their prey. They were trained attack dogs, not hunting dogs. Unlike the jimis, they had not raved and ranted during the attack on the warthog. They had not uttered a single bark during the whole chase, and they were dead silent now. The jimis would have made enough noise to scare the whole forest. The jimis would have been easy to follow. But the Alsatians were impossible to follow in the thick forest.

I limped on, calling for Nigel with mounting alarm. The forest was dead still. Darkness was closing in fast.

I walked on. Lighting flashed, throwing grotesque shadows into the trees around me. A sudden thunderclap echoed eerily through the undergrowth.

I was petrified with fear.

I was about to turn round and run home when I heard a muffled sound in the undergrowth and stopped to listen.

The forest was quite still. A sharp cry cut into the night, a frightened sound that sounded like a sheep that was about to have its throat cut.

Then silence.

"Nigel?" I called out. "Is that you, Nigel?"

There was no reply. I heard stealthy movements up ahead. Then silence. Fear tore at my stomach — a cold, screaming fear that filled my mouth and made it impossible to breathe. I moved on slowly. It was nearly dark now.

Lightning lit up the night, blinding and illuminating at the same time. In its terrible light, I saw a large black thing lying on the ground.

I stopped. My fear told me to run home and get help. But my mind told me no villager would dare go in the forest after dark. The soldiers had warned us against it. The soldiers had made it very clear that anyone found in the forest after dark would be shot dead.

I approached the thing lying there on the ground. Then I recognized it.

It was the body of fearless old Pepper, and he was dead. His head was split wide open, and there was blood all around him.

I cried out with fear. I ran in panicked circles and called Nigel's name until the forest rang with it and I was hoarse from yelling. I got no reply.

I ran back the way we had come and tried to find my way home. I had to get some help. If Old Moses could do so much harm to such a big dog, I needed all the help I could find. Forgetting the wound in my foot, I ran like the wind. The river was rising when I crossed back into the village. I got home long after dark, scratched and battered by the trees I had run into in the dark, and frightened like I had never been before.

Father was still at work and Hari was not at home. Mother sat alone by the fireplace worrying about us all.

"Where have you been?" she asked me. "I have worried about you all evening."

"Nowhere," I said.

I did not know how to tell her that I had lost the white boy in the forest. I was not supposed to go in the forest in the first place. I was not supposed to be with the white boy either. So, in the end, I told her nothing. I had been nowhere and had done nothing with no one, as usual.

She looked me in the face, saw the fear in my eyes and said, "Wait until your father gets home. Then you will tell him where you have been all day."

I was tempted to run back to the forest and stay there until I had found Nigel. But I could not go back alone. It frightened me just thinking about it.

I knew of only one person who could go into the forest so late at night.

"Where is Hari?" I asked.

My mother regarded me with renewed interest.

"Where have you been?" she asked.

"Nowhere."

Throughout dinner I thought about my predicament. Dozens of desperate thoughts went through my head, and all of them were terrifying. I could not eat or sit still. I went outside the hut several times and thought seriously of drowning myself in the river. I thought of going to Bwana Ruin's. Instead I sat trembling and hoping my mother would not notice.

But she did. She watched me stew in my own terror.

"Kariuki," she asked again. "What have you been up to?"

"Nothing."

About an hour later, my father came to ask whether I had seen the little white man that day. The rain was starting and his white uniform was dotted with dark raindrops. He looked so miserable that he frightened me.

I told my father I had not seen the white boy at all that day.

"Where could he be?" he asked.

"I don't know," I said.

He went back to the farmhouse looking more miserable than ever. My mother watched me intently. She stared at me with that all-seeing and all-knowing look, and I was afraid she had seen me sneak into the forest with Nigel.

I was on the verge of confessing everything to her

when Father suddenly came home and told us the little white man was missing.

"The dogs too," he told us. "Bwana Ruin has called the army."

I lay awake that night, listening to the thunder crash and the rain beat down in earnest. I decided I would wake up before dawn and go back to the forest and find Nigel. I would search the whole forest. I would not eat or rest. I would not return until I had found Nigel.

Then a desperate thought entered my mind. What if I did not find Nigel? What then?

I would run away from home, I said to myself. I would go far, far away and stay there. I would go over the Loldaiga hills to the land of the Dorobos and change my name. I would go where no one would ever find me. I would never return home if I did not find Nigel.

By dawn the village was surrounded by an army of angry white soldiers. They rounded all of us up and herded us into the auction pen. The rain during the night had turned it into a mud pool. They made us sit on the mud while they went through our huts as before.

This time they were not looking for guns or for the mau-mau. They were looking for clues that would link the villagers to the disappearance of the white boy. However, this time they unearthed things that would send a lot of people to detention for a long, long time. They found things for which some villagers would no doubt be hanged.

They found a homemade gun and three rounds of

ammunition. They found stolen maps and medical sup-
plies — things that illiterate villagers were not supposed
to know anything about.

Then they called the villagers out one by one and
marched them to the farmhouse. Bwana Ruin had set
up an interrogation office in a tent on his front lawn.
They were ordered to produce their identity cards, their
movement passes and their work permits. They were
asked whether they or anyone they knew was mau-
mau. Some of them were released right away and
allowed to go back to their homes. Others were herded
to one side under the watchful eyes of the soldiers.

Then my turn came for questioning. I limped into the
tent and stood in front of the table set up there. Behind
the table were Bwana Ruin and three white officers.

The questioning was done by a serious-looking
officer with gray hair and grave, old eyes. He asked what
had happened to my foot. I told him that I had stepped
on a thorn. He asked me how old I was. I told him. He
wanted to know where I went to school. I told him that
too. The soldiers had found a toy pistol in my mother's
hut. He showed it to me and asked if I knew what it was.
I told him.

"Do you know where we found it?" he asked me.

"Under my bed," I said. "I put it there."

He glanced at Bwana Ruin. The old man was sitting
slumped in his chair with an angry frown on his face.

"Whose gun is it?" the inspector asked me.

"It is mine," I told him.

"Yours, *aye*?" Bwana Ruin sat up. "Where did you get it from?"

"Nigel gave it to me," I told him. "The Bwana Kidogo gave it to me."

"He did, did he?" Bwana Ruin asked me. "Whose *toto* are you, *aye*? Whose child are you?"

The inspector interrupted him to ask me when exactly the Bwana Kidogo had given me the gun. I could not remember exactly when. But it was after we got tired of playing cowboys and discovered hunting. It all seemed so long ago now.

"So you are a friend of the Bwana Kidogo?" he asked me.

I answered that I was.

"When did you see him last?" he asked.

I hesitated. What did they know? Had someone found out about our hunting expedition with Salt and Pepper? Nigel would never have told anyone about it. That was our understanding.

"Yesterday," I said to the inspector.

"Where did you last see him?"

"When the soldiers came to surround us," I said to him. "He was standing over there with mamsab."

Among the suspects waiting to be taken away to Nanyuki for further investigation was Hari. I saw him sitting on the grass with other suspects while armed soldiers stood guard over them. When our eyes met he looked right through me. I realized I was not supposed to know him.

I turned to the inspector and answered his questions as best as I could. When the questioning was over, the inspector said I could go back home. My mother was there, worried as I had never seen her worried before.

"I told you," she said gravely. "Your father told you all the time too."

"Told me what?" I asked her.

"To keep away from the little white man. Now see what misfortune you have brought upon us all."

"But it is not my fault," I said.

"Whose fault is it?" she asked, her voice full of pain.

"I don't know."

"You don't know, you don't know," she said, close to tears. "When will you ever know anything?"

I had no idea. Nobody ever told me anything that was not an order. But the very first opportunity I got, I called Jimi and together we sneaked out of the village and down through the forest to the river. We forded the swollen river, way downstream from the village, and set out to look for Nigel.

We covered a lot of ground that day. Starting from where I had left off the night before, we worked our way up the valley, searching under every bush and tree. We found the body of the other Alsatian about a mile away from the first, big and bloated and beginning to smell. He had died from two deep cuts on his head, and there were blue flies all around him. The area bore the signs of a fierce fight, and there was blood all over.

I was really scared now. Jimi whined from fear. I had

never seen him so terrified. It took all the promises I could make to persuade him to stay with me a little longer.

My foot hurt terribly. It ached with every step I took, and I had to stop every now and then to rest it. I cut a stick to lean on, and we continued our search. I called out Nigel's name. Jimi barked out Nigel's name. We stopped, listened, then moved on.

Sometimes we came across a human footprint. Sometimes a broken twig was all that was left to tell us that something, or someone, had been there. We came across a herd of buffalo browsing their way quietly through a glade.

I knew we had nothing to fear from the herd. Only a lone or a wounded buffalo was dangerous. I led Jimi quietly around the glade. They saw us and snorted a warning at us to keep our distance.

We searched in countless caves along the river valley. We found nothing but bat droppings and old animal lairs.

In the late afternoon we called off the search and returned tiredly home. Along the way, we came upon a party of white soldiers searching for Nigel's body along the river bank. They thought he might have gone fishing and drowned in a flash flood.

When we got back home, we found soldiers about to arrest my father. They had him in handcuffs and were preparing to take him away.

"Don't cry," he said to my mother.

I had never seen my mother weep. She had suffered enough in her life, but I had never seen her shed a tear. The closest she had ever come to crying was when my little sister died of measles. Now, as the soldiers prepared to take my father away, she put her arm around me and drew me to her. He seemed to notice me then.

"Where have you been?" he asked.

"Nowhere," I said.

"Stay with your mother," he ordered. "And do not cry."

I was too frightened to cry. It seemed that my life had been turned upside down. Nothing was the same. Even my own father, Bwana Ruin's most important man and the toughest, bravest man I knew, was not immune to the terror that had suddenly descended on us. Worse still, he seemed to have resigned himself to being shot.

They took him roughly by the arm and led him away. Even Jimi seemed to understand what was happening. He whined faintly and crawled under the grain store to hide.

"Where are they taking him?" I asked my mother.

"I don't know," she told me.

"Will they hang him?"

"I don't know."

We watched them until they disappeared among the village huts.

"What happened to your foot?" my mother finally asked.

"Nothing," I replied.

"You run to the river and fetch some water," she said. "We have a lot of washing to do today."

It was very late in the afternoon and there was not enough sun left in the sky to dry any clothes. I did not understand why she wanted to do her washing at this time of day. But I took the bucket and obediently limped down to the place where I had first met the little white man.

There was no joy in it any more. There was no joy in anything any more.

Ten

THE SOLDIERS DID not find Nigel's body in the river. The soldiers did not find Nigel's body anywhere. Everyone was sad or frightened, and the whole farm was covered in a cloud of gloom.

The following day, my father and Hari were released from prison. They came home late in the morning tired and very hungry. They did not wish to talk about their experiences.

I left them waiting for an early lunch of ugali and sour milk and sneaked out of the village to continue the search for my lost friend. Jimi completely refused to come with me. He did not like what was going on in the forest any more than I did. Finding the Alsatian's bloated body had seriously affected his confidence. So I resumed the search alone.

I started where we had called it off the day before and worked my way up river along the forest. I crawled into each and every cave and animal lair I came across. I looked everywhere, even up in the trees, hoping against hope that I would find the white boy alive and unharmed.

It had rained heavily the night before, so there was little chance of finding any trail more than a few hours old.

I came across several fresh animal prints. One was a lone buffalo's. One appeared to have been left by a lion or a very large dog. There were many smaller prints left by gazelles and other deer. But I came across no human trail.

It occured to me then that Nigel might have been killed and eaten by wild animals. But then I would have found remnants — his shoes or his clothing.

My foot was swollen and full of pus. It was extremely painful, and I had to stop several times to rest it. Finally, I used a dry thorn to prick the wound. I squeezed out all the pus, wrapped the foot in a rag torn from my shirt tail and moved on.

I searched all morning. I went deeper and farther into the forest than I had ever been before. I discovered caves and hide-outs I did not know existed, where foxes hid their cubs and wild cats had litters of kittens. Once I came upon a wild dog carrying a freshly killed dik-dik back to its lair.

Then, late in the afternoon, I found caves that showed signs of human occupation. There were fireplaces and cooking things. There were footprints all over and animal bones left behind when the occupants had moved on.

It was in the last of the caves that I found Nigel. There were hot embers in the fireplace and piles of deer and sheep skins against the wall. There was a pile of firewood at one end. There were cooking pots and machetes and spears and countless other things. The smell of buffalo meat was everywhere.

Nigel was at the very deep end of the cave, tied up and covered with several large sheep skins. At first I thought he was dead.

I removed the sheep skins and turned him over. Then he blinked at me, and I knew he was alive.

He was really black now, covered in soot and dust, and he smelled of skins.

I untied him and removed the gag from his mouth.

"Rookie," he said. "Now I know where my grandfather's sheep disappear to."

"Are you all right?" I asked.

He was unharmed, he told me. But he was very hungry.

"I did not know where to look for you," I told him. "I searched the whole forest. Who brought you here?"

"Some people," Nigel said.

"What sort of people?"

He had not seen them at all. They had covered his head with a sack and kept him under the sheep skins.

I was overjoyed to find him alive. Now my father and brother Hari would not have to hang. Maybe things could go back to being normal again. I led him out of the cave.

"What happened to your foot?" he asked.

"A thorn," I told him. "Let's go home now."

He gave me his shoulder to lean on. I put my arm around him and we descended into the river valley. It was late afternoon. The clouds were getting ready for another downpour.

As we hurried through the undergrowth, I told Nigel how I had worried about him, how the whole village was in turmoil over his disappearance, and how the army was out looking for him.

"I thought you were dead," I told him.

"So did I," he told me. "But I knew you would find me."

He told me how he had run on into the forest and found Pepper lying on the ground with a deep cut on his head. It had scared him to his stomach. Then, as he had turned to run back the way he had come, someone had thrown a sack over his head and carried him screaming into the forest. He had heard my desperate calls, but by then they had gagged him and he could not call back.

"Did they beat you?" I asked.

They had not. But he had thought they were going to kill him.

"They are really strange people," he told me.

I knew that to be true. Why else would they be called the men of the forest and live there with wild animals? Why else would they steal Nigel and hide him in a cave?

We were about a mile from the cave, walking along

the river valley, when it happened. We did not see or hear them at all.

The first thing we knew, we were pinned to the ground and they were tying our hands behind our backs. Then they lifted us to our feet and rushed us back to the cave.

There were eight of them. Eight of the biggest, wildest men I had ever seen, and they smelled of buffalo. Among them were men I had seen before in the village and the men that had given me the message to take to Hari. The one with the scar was there too, the one who had said they would cut my tongue out if I ever talked to anyone about them.

They carried us deep inside the cave and tied our legs and gagged us. Then they covered us with the sheep skins and returned to the fireside to discuss our fate.

We were a big problem, it appeared. They did not seem to know exactly what to do with us. They discussed us for a long time.

"Let's kill them," I heard one of them say.

"Kill Hari's brother?" another one asked. "Hari would not like that."

"Hari does not have to like it. Hari did not do as we agreed. So we can kill his brother too."

"They are only boys," said another voice. "They are not circumcised."

I had heard that the mau-mau did not kill uncircumcised boys. There was hope for us.

They talked about the soldiers. The soldiers were back in the forest and it worried some of them. They wanted to leave for the mountains as fast as possible.

"We must wait for Cutter-Cutter," one of them said. "We must wait for the others. Then we will know what to do. But we must not kill the boys. It is bad luck to kill uncircumcised boys."

Then they talked about other things, about guns and about a liberation war. I did not understand half the things they said.

We lay under the skins for a long time. We heard them talk and move in and out of the cave. But no one came to tell us anything. They roasted meat and ate it. They did not give us any and left us exactly where we were.

Hours later their friends arrived. They held a long and heated discussion. Then we were dragged from under the skins. They removed the gags from our mouths and untied our legs. They led us to the entrance.

It was raining outside and the newcomers were wet through and through. Hari stepped out from among them, looking haggard and defeated, and he regarded me for a long moment before he spoke to me.

His tortured face said it all. This time I had gone too far.

"Little brother," he said. "You have placed me in a very desperate predicament."

He had never called me little brother before. It

scared me more than the anticipation of his left-right slaps.

"A very difficult position," he repeated.

"How?" I asked.

"What are you doing here?" he asked.

"I came to find Nigel."

"Why?" There was pain in his voice.

"I lost him."

He looked from me to the men as if to say, "I told you."

Then he turned to the white boy, regarded him with pity, and appeared about to say something. He shook his head and turned to me instead. He studied me for a long, long moment. He was breathing hard as fury built up inside him.

Then he hit me.

The left-right caught me unawares. It rocked my head from side to side and left my whole body vibrating through and through.

He had never hit me so hard before. The blow left me wordless and tearless.

"Why?" he asked.

"He is my friend," I said.

His face was contorted with fury. He made a fist and pulled it back to strike again. He had never hit me with his fist. I was certain he would kill me this time.

Then Nigel lashed out with his boot and kicked Hari in the shins.

No one was more surprised by this foolhardy move than Hari himself. He looked from me to Nigel. His face was full of humiliated anger. He raised his hand to strike at Nigel. I was certain the blow would kill him.

"Stop it," I yelled. "Don't hit him."

Hari turned from Nigel to me. He appeared thoroughly confused and embarrassed. He considered which one of us to hit first. His friends watched with great interest. Cutter-Cutter was smiling quietly.

Finally, Hari lowered his fist and said, "What shall I do with you?"

"Let us go home," I said. "We'll never come to the forest again."

He looked from us to Cutter-Cutter. Cutter-Cutter looked on, let him make all the decisions.

"I can't let you go," he said. "It is not that simple."

Cutter-Cutter gave a signal and the men grabbed us. They tied our hands and legs again and returned us to the back of the cave. Then they tried to decide what to do with us.

I was glad Nigel did not understand our language. He would have died of fright if he had understood some of the things the men were suggesting.

They discussed us for a long time.

"Let them go home," Hari said at last.

"Because he is your brother?" Cutter-Cutter asked.

"Your plan cannot work now," Hari told them. "The forest is full of soldiers already. They are looking everywhere for the white boy."

They were quiet for a moment, thinking. But I could also tell there was fear in the air.

"Let us kill the little white man," the scarred one said.

"No," Hari said quickly.

"Why not?"

"There is nothing to be gained by that. It will only make them angrier. Besides, he is only a boy. And that was not the plan."

"The plan," Cutter-Cutter said quietly. "The plan was that you would take the note to the white man."

"I had no chance," Hari told him.

"Then you will take the note to him?" Cutter-Cutter asked.

"I never said that I would not," Hari answered. "It is just that I had no chance. They have arrested me twice already. They let me out of prison just this morning."

"Did they torture you?" someone asked.

Hari snorted angrily. "What do you think? I told them nothing."

They were quiet for a long time after that. Later on they were joined by another gang. The new group brought news that there were even more soldiers in the forest around the farm.

They were all afraid and restless now. They discussed what they should do. They discussed for a long time.

"Here is what we shall do," Cutter-Cutter finally told them. "Hari will take the note and go back to the farm. He will give the note to the white man. Then, when Hari confirms that he has done so, we shall take the boys and go up to the mountains. We shall go there and give the *mzungu* time to make up his mind."

They sounded agreed on this course of action. Then Hari spoke up.

"It will not work," he told them.

"Why not?" Cutter-Cutter asked impatiently.

"I don't think the *mzungu* will give up the land in exchange for two little boys," he said. "Believe me, I know him."

"Then we shall kill the little white man," Cutter-Cutter said. "We shall kill his grandson and see how he likes that."

I was cold with terror. I struggled silently trying to free my hands. Nigel was doing the same thing and not being any more successful than I was. After a while we gave up and lay back to await our fate. We listened to the men talk.

"Rookie?" Nigel whispered to me. "What are they talking about?"

"They are talking about us," I told him. "They want to kill us."

"Why?" he asked me.

"They want Bwana Ruin's farm," I told him. "They want your grandfather's land."

"Why?"

I told him I did not know. They said that it was their land, that Bwana Ruin was a foreigner and had stolen it from them.

"They are liars," Nigel whispered back. "My grandfather is not a thief."

That was what I thought too. But they said that it was their land and they would kill us if Bwana Ruin did not do as they demanded.

Nigel digested that information for a while.

"Rookie?" he asked finally. "What shall we do?"

I had no idea. They would definitely kill us. There was no doubt in my mind about that.

But they did not kill us right away. First, at Hari's insistence, they took us out and fed us roast buffalo meat. We ate hungrily. When we had finished, they gave us mugs of hot buffalo broth. They fed us very well, considering what they intended to do with us. Then they tied us up again and took us back under the pile of skins.

I must have fallen asleep after that. A deep, deep sleep with dreams of hunting and fishing.

I was surprised when I woke up to find myself under the skins, tied up hand and foot. It was the biting pain in my foot that woke me up.

The cave was dead quiet. Nigel slept peacefully by my side, breathing easily. I lay for a long time wondering what time of day it was and what the people of the forest were doing. My foot throbbed with every heartbeat. The first chance I got I would squeeze out the pus once again. Then I would put salt on the wound. I knew of many forest plants that were good medicine for wounds. But they were impossibly far away now.

I heard a creeping movement in the cave. I pricked my ears and listened. The movement was quick and quiet and very worrying.

Then the sheep skins were pulled away from us and I saw a shadow looming over us. It had a machete in one hand and appeared ready to strike.

I thought this was the moment of our death. I opened my mouth to scream but no sound came out. I fought back, kicked out at the shadow.

"Kariuki," the shadow barked. "Be still."

It was Hari. While I sighed with relief, he bent down and cut the ropes that bound our hands and feet. Then he pulled us to our feet and dragged us out to the mouth of the cave.

"You must go away from here," he said urgently. "You must go home now."

The others had gone up to the mountain, he told us. Their plan had failed. There were too many soldiers in the forest looking for Nigel. Cutter-Cutter had changed his mind about killing us. He was a superstitious man and had decided to leave us there in the cave for the hyenas and the wild dogs.

The rain had stopped. I could tell from the position of the sun that it was about noon. Sunlight glinted on the wet leaves.

I sat down to squeeze the pus out of my wound. It was an extremely painful exercise, but my foot felt much better afterwards. I wrapped it in rags once more.

"Go that way," Hari said, pointing south. "The soldiers are not far from here. They will show you the way home."

"What about you?" I asked him.

"I can't come back home."

"Why not?" I asked in panic. "You are not one of them. You are my brother."

"I must follow my friends," he said. "Don't worry about me. I will be all right. One day I'll come back home and be with you."

I was almost in tears.

"Go now," he said to us. "Go quickly in case they come back and find you here. Hurry home and stay there."

He turned to Nigel. He regarded him for a long moment.

"It was my idea to bring you here," he said. "I'm sorry." There was pain in his voice.

"Don't play in the forest again," he said to Nigel. "The forest is not safe any more. Not for little white men. Not for anyone."

Then he gave us a shove and we were off. We went stumbling down the hill until we came to the thicker undergrowth and slowed down. Nigel gave me his shoulder to lean on. We plunged into the undergrowth, walking fast and urgently, eager to put as much distance between us and the hide-out as possible.

Eleven

WE MET THE soldiers about a mile from the hide-out, stalking through the wet bush as silently as ghosts. We did not know they were there until we found ourselves in the midst of a dozen grim faces, their guns pointed at us.

They were happy to see Nigel alive and well.

"Where have you been?" they asked.

"In the forest," he told them. "Rookie found me."

He told them how he had been kidnapped by the men with spears. How they had taken him from one hide-out to the next until he had lost all sense of direction. And how I had found him and rescued him.

The officer in charge wanted to know how many terrorists there were. We gave them all the information we could. There were about twenty men and they were headed for the mountains. He gave us four soldiers to escort us home and led the rest of them after the gang.

The soldiers rushed us on through the forest. They got us home in the late afternoon. When we came to the farm, they took Nigel to his grandparents and left me to find my way back to the village.

Father was home, pacing the yard and talking distractedly to himself. For a moment he did not seem to remember me. Then he recognized me and pounced on me. He lifted me off my feet and shook me violently.

"Where have you been?" he asked.

"Nowhere," I told him. "Put me down."

He put me down. But he did not let go of my collar. His eyes were wild, his face old and contorted.

"Where have you been?" he demanded.

"In the forest."

He raised his fist to strike me. Then he saw Mother watching from the doorway and stopped. He lowered his fist but held onto my collar.

"We did not sleep at all last night," he told me. "Your mother was so worried about you and Hari."

I told him that I had seen Hari. He was on his way to the mountains with his friends from the forest.

I had never seen my father so angry and confused. And under the anger and the confusion I saw fear. The fear of new and unknown terrors. The fear that had first invaded the village with the disappearance of Bwana Ruin's gun and the arrival of the white soldiers. Fear of something so large and so terrible it had neither face nor name.

I had finally lost him his job. I wanted to drown myself.

"You must not tell the soldiers about Hari," he told me. "You must not talk about the people of the forest to anyone. Do you understand? You must not tell them about your brother Hari."

But I already had. We had told the soldiers in the forest exactly where to find him.

Father's face collapsed when he heard this news. His eyes lost all the life in them, and his hand slipped from my collar and flopped dead by his side.

I was petrified. To alleviate the pain, I reported that I had found the boy.

"Found the boy?" he asked. "What boy?"

"Nigel," I told him.

"Najo?"

He tried to remember where he had heard the name.

They had treated him cruelly in jail. Much later, when he was no longer so afraid and could talk about it, I learned that they had tortured him to reveal his connections with the mau-mau. Someone had told them that he was the leader of the mau-mau. Someone had told the police that my father conducted oathing ceremonies at night and gave food to the mau-mau. The soldiers had tried to make him confess to things he knew nothing about. They had also tried to make him admit to murdering the white boy.

"Who is Najo?" he asked.

"The white boy," I told him. "The Bwana Kidogo."

It took a lot of effort to remember. But he finally did. He seemed revived by the information.

"You found the boy?" he asked doubtfully.

"Yes, Father."

"Where did you find him?"

"In the forest."

He paused thoughtfully.

"Is he dead?"

"No, Father," I told him. "Nigel is alive."

He rapped my head with his knuckles. Why had I told him the little white man was dead? I hadn't. They must have scared him a lot when they locked him in prison.

"The white boy is alive," I said to him.

"Where is he?" he demanded.

"He went home."

He turned and rushed off to see for himself. I was left stranded in the yard between the hut and the grain store, uncertain which way to go. My mother watched me from the doorway of the hut. Her eyes were full of sadness and pity.

"Are you hungry?" she asked.

I was not hungry.

"I'll make some ugali," she said.

After a while, my father came back and told me not to worry, that they had found the white boy. Bwana Ruin had said that my father could now go back to work in the kitchen.

He did not seem to know what else to say to me. He raised his hand absent-mindedly over my head. I braced myself for a rapping with the knuckles. His hand opened up and landed palm down on my head.

"Good," he said, patting me gently on the head. "Good."

Then he turned and walked away.

I sat there for a long time and tried to understand what was happening to my quiet life. I had found Nigel and brought him safely back to his grandfather. I was only now beginning to realize what it all meant. As soon as Nigel told them how, and by whom, he had been kidnapped, the soldiers would come back and take us all out and hang us.

Jimi saw I was miserable and crawled from under the grain store to lie by my side. We sat quietly for a long time.

Then Nigel suddenly showed up in our yard. Mother nearly collapsed from anxiety when she saw him. Father came to talk to him, but the words would not leave his mouth, and he went away muttering to himself in a language the white boy could not understand.

"Rookie," Nigel said, "why is everybody so sad?"

"I don't know."

His grandfather wanted to talk to me, he told me. To thank me for saving his grandson's life. I was not entirely happy about the whole thing, but I went with him.

Jimi followed us as far as the gate to the big farmhouse. Then he remembered that Salt and Pepper lived there, and he ran back to the village.

Bwana Ruin met us on the veranda of the house. He took my arm and patted me gently on the head the way my father had done. He showed us to the end of the veranda where tea was set for two and went away.

Mamsab Ruin served us tea and cakes and sat back

to watch us eat. She studied me just as closely as the villagers had studied Nigel when he ate ugali at my mother's house. It was almost as though she expected me to find it revolting.

She was older than Bwana Ruin and more frail and all gray. I had heard it said that she was the real owner of the farm and that Bwana Ruin had married her because she was rich.

Nigel told me the bodies of the dead dogs had been recovered and brought back to the farm. They had been buried in the family graveyard by the orchard. Then Nigel gave me back the toy gun the soldiers had taken from under my bed. I took the gun, but I knew that I would have to throw it in the latrine when I got back home.

As I left to go back to the village, Bwana Ruin came to inform us that the soldiers had returned. The search for the terrorists had been called off for the moment. The soldiers had completely lost their quarry. But they had found one terrorist and wanted our assistance in identifying him.

He took us to the auction pen where the dead man lay half naked and spread-eagled on the grass. He was covered in blood and mud and was a ghastly sight to see.

We stepped forward to look at his face.

My body was suddenly numb.

"Do you recognize this man?" the officer in charge asked us.

There were tears in my eyes. I could neither see nor speak.

"Do you know this man?" the officer asked again, raising his voice.

I choked on the reply. Nigel looked helplessly at me.

"Nigel?" his grandfather warned.

"Yes," Nigel said. "We saw him."

"Was he one of them?" the officer asked.

"I don't know," Nigel said nervously.

"Nigel," Bwana Ruin barked. "Answer the officer's question properly. Was he or was he not one of the terrorists?"

The officer glanced at Bwana Ruin with disapproval.

"Nigel," he said gently. "I want you to think very hard before you answer this question. Was this not one of the men who kidnapped you?"

"No, sir," Nigel said right away.

"Think, Nigel," the officer said patiently. "Think. You have just told me that you know this man."

"Yes, sir," Nigel said.

"From where do you know this man?" the officer asked.

"From here on the farm," Nigel said. "He is the man who runs the dairy."

Bwana Ruin grunted angrily. The officer glanced at him, then back at Nigel.

"Nigel," he said. "Was this man in the forest at all when you were there?"

"Yes," Nigel answered. "He is the man who set us free."

"Nigel." Bwana Ruin sounding impatient. "The truth, Nigel. Nothing but the truth."

"That's the truth, Grandpa."

"But you told me that your... that this native boy rescued you," Bwana Ruin said.

"Yes, Grandpa," Nigel told him. "First my friend found me and set me free. Then they caught us and took us back to the cave and tied us up again. Then this man came and set us free."

"How did he find you?" the officer asked.

"He did not say, sir," Nigel answered.

"Did he tell you what he was doing there in the forest?" the officer asked.

"We did not ask, sir," Nigel answered.

The officer was not at all satisfied. He turned to glare at me. He took me by the shoulder, squeezing hard, and asked me if I knew the dead man.

I clenched my teeth and bit back the sobs that were rising up inside me.

"Answer me," the officer barked.

I could only nod.

"Do you know his name?" he asked.

"Hari," I sobbed. "He is my brother Hari."

Then I turned and ran off back to the village. I skirted my mother's house and ran through the bush down to the river.

Only then did I stop running. My foot was on fire and my head was in turmoil.

What had I done? What should I do? What would

happen now that everything was in chaos and it was all my fault?

I limped along the river path I had walked so many times with Hari when he taught me how to bait the hooks with live worms and grasshoppers. Seeing nothing and hearing nothing, I walked slowly up the path until I came to the duck pool where I had first met the people of the forest. Where they had first given me a message for Hari. Where they had warned me never to tell the soldiers about them.

Would they know that I had told? What would happen to me then?

I climbed down the bank to the water's edge. The river had gone down a little but the water was thick with driftwood and red mud from the mountain floods. I could just make it to my special place under the cliff and sit down by the pool.

The water roared and frothed. It rushed leaves and branches down river in a mad frenzy and lapped at my toes as it passed under me.

Any minute now a flash flood would come and wash me down the river along with the driftwood and drown me. I sat on the wet rocks and waited for it to happen.

It was then that the tears came. I cried till my chest hurt and there were no more tears left to shed. Unable to stop myself, I went on weeping, sobbing hard, dry sobs. The pain in my heart was greater than any pain I had ever experienced. Worse than any beating I had ever endured from Hari or anyone else. Many times worse than anything I had ever received from Lesson One.

A family of colobus monkeys came swinging through the trees, their babies clinging to their bellies. I saw them pass but I did not care, and they went away up the river, eating their way through the mokoe trees and wondering why I did not call out to them today.

Then Nigel found me. He came crashing down from the bank and hopped from rock to rock and sat down next to me.

We were silent for a long time and let the river do the talking. We did not utter a single word until it was nearly dark and the cold rose from the river like smoke from a dying fire.

"Rookie," Nigel said finally. "I'm sorry about your brother."

I nodded. When I tried to smile, tears came back to my eyes. I shut my eyes tight and saw Hari lying dead on the ground with bullet holes in his chest. The sobs came again and I clenched my teeth until they had passed.

"He was my best friend," I said to Nigel.

I had told him everything about me and Hari. Hari had taught me to fish. Hari had taught me to hunt. Hari had taught me everything I knew.

Then Nigel put his arm around my shoulder and the dam burst. I cried uncontrollably. It took me a long time to calm down.

We sat and listened to the river roar. The level was

rising and my feet were now under the cold, numbing water. The pain had subsided.

Then the ducks came floating down the river, as silent as the leaves, and we turned to watch them. There were only three of them now, the mother duck and two of her ducklings. They moved around the pool, looking apprehensively over their backs as they fed on the few insects they could catch. They had never seen Nigel, and they were nervous. But Nigel did not throw stones at them. Like me, he just sat and watched.

I told him about the duck family. I told him how we had been friends for a long, long time. I had known the mother duck long before the ducklings were hatched and she had always trusted me. I wondered what had happened to the father duck and the other ducklings. The pool was not the same without them. The forest was not the same without them.

Everything had changed. The forest was now full of new and strange shadows and sounds that I could not understand.

After a few swims round the pool, the mother duck led her surviving ducklings away down the river, floating on the water and letting the current carry them.

"Rookie," Nigel cried suddenly. "The river."

The water had risen up to our knees without us noticing. We heard a loud rumbling up river as the floods swept down from the mountains. We scrambled from there and clambered up the bank to the fishermen's path.

We got out of the water just in time. The flood rounded the bend, roaring like thunder and crashing down everything that stood in its path. It swept past where we stood terrified, carrying dead animals and logs and debris downstream. The forest watched and trembled. Nothing was safe any more.

"Lean on me," Nigel said.

I put my arm around his shoulder. He lifted my side and took the weight off my injured foot.

That was how we returned to the village, shoulder to shoulder, down the fishermen's path with the flood waters roaring furiously below us.

The Mzungu Boy is a work of fiction that takes place in Kenya, Africa, in the early 1950s. At that time the country, a British colony, was faced with an uprising that became known as the Mau Mau Rebellion. Much of Kenya, including the best farmland, was in the hands of European settlers. At best, native Kenyans were allowed to work on the land as tenant farmers, under exploitative and demeaning conditions. The rebels wanted the white settlers to leave the country so native Africans could have their independence. As the uprising gained momentum, British rulers declared a state of emergency. Troops set out to arrest Mau Mau leaders, and rebel groups took to hiding in the forests.

By the end of 1959, most of the Mau Mau guerillas had been wiped out, and the state of emergency was lifted. Casualties were estimated to be well over 12,000, virtually all native Africans.

Kenya became an independent country on December 12, 1963. Today it has a population of 32 million people.

MEJA MWANGI was born in Nanyuki, in central Kenya, in 1948. He has worked in film and television as a director, casting director and screenwriter, and he is the author of several novels and children's books, including *The Last*

Plague, Striving for the Wind, Kill Me Quick and *Going Down River Road*. His books have been translated into several languages, including Basque, German, French, Russian and Japanese. *The Mzungu Boy* won the prestigious Deutsche Jungendliteraturpreis when it was first published in 1990.